I0668847

FANGS
of the
SEA

AIRSHIP 27 PRODUCTIONS

™

Fangs of the Sea
© 2021 Fred Adams Jr.

Published by Airship 27 Productions
www.airship27.com
www.airship27hangar.com

Interior illustrations © 2021 Rob Davis
Cover illustration © 2021 Adam Benet Shaw

Editor: Ron Fortier
Associate Editor: Jonathan Sweet
Marketing and Promotions Manager: Michael Vance
Production designer: Rob Davis

All rights reserved under International and Pan-American Copyright Conventions. No part of this book may be reproduced in any manner without permission in writing from the copyright holder, except by a reviewer, who may quote brief passages in a review.

ISBN: 978-1-953589-04-0

Printed in the United States of America

10 9 8 7 6 5 4 3 2 1

FANGS of the SEA

by Fred Adams Jr.

1

Mateo cast his net into the sea again. Fishing had been poor the past few nights, but he and his companions labored on in the hope that just as the weather changed, so might the catch. Life was not difficult on the little island of Armonía, but it required a regular discipline cultivated by more than a century of occupation. Mateo's great-great-grandparents were part of a band of faithful Catholics horrified by the tactics of the Inquisition. They fled Spain before they could be dragged before the *auto-da-fes* and tortured to death. A small group of five islands to the south of Cuba offered the chance for a new start, and they had managed a peaceful existence there ever since. Their numbers had never been large, but they were industrious and made a good life for themselves.

As a wave dragged across the sand, Mateo felt a tug at his net. Whatever he had caught was heavy. He called to Alejandro and Lucas to help him.

"What have you got, Mateo? A dolphin? A shark?" Lucas said.

Alejandro snorted. "More likely a log. When did you ever see a dolphin in such shallow water?"

"Let's pull in the net and find out." Mateo set his feet in the sand and tugged at the line. In the pre-dawn light, they saw the net with a good-sized bulk wrapped inside the mesh emerge from a receding wave.

Mateo splashed through the surf toward the net. "*Madre Dios.* It is a man."

He reached the net and peered through the ropes.

"Is he alive?" Alejandro said.

"He looks to be dead." Mateo raised his hand to his forehead to cross himself but froze as the corpse's eyes sprang open, glowing a dark crimson. Before he could speak or move, a hand with talons like knives slashed through the net and in the same swipe opened Mateo's belly. The fisherman clutched at the exposed loops of gut, desperate to hold them in. With a snarl, the creature tore free from the net and grabbed Mateo by the shoulders, clamping his fanged jaw on the pulsing jugular, sucking down the rich, red blood.

Suddenly, the surf was alive with men but not men, boiling out of the waves and running through the surf toward the fishermen. Red-eyed devils they were, fangs bared, their limbs festooned with rags and seaweed.

With their arms wrapped in the lines of the net, Alejandro and Lucas could not turn and run, but it was no matter. The things from the sea were upon them in seconds.

Two of them leapt on Lucas, sinking their claws into his body and savaging him with their fangs. Others, maddened by the scent of gore joined in as their companions all but tore Alejandro's head from his neck, ripping, slashing, and feasting on his pulsing blood. Others bit deep into thighs and arms searching for a vein.

When the sun rose, the beach was quiet again, and the incoming tide washed the gore from the mangled fishermen as the sea went about its business, eternal and uncaring. Little fish, drawn by the blood in the water, nibbled at the raw edges of wounds as the fins of their larger brethren circled thirty yards out, frustrated by the shallow water, waiting for the tide to lift the bodies and pull them out to sea or give them the depth to approach. Mother Ocean was a good provider. One need only be patient.

Sebastian de la Vega, the *jefe* of the only village on Armonía was at his breakfast. He was reading a book he had borrowed from Father Beppo, priest of the Catholic church on Cuerpo Santo, the nearby island that was the center of the five-island exile colony. A few hundred souls, almost completely self-sufficient, having little to do with the outside world. Books were rare, and although he had read it twice before, Sebastian still found surprises in every chapter of the adventures of Don Quixote. His delicacy of manner hinted at aristocratic origins maintained in the face of a hardscrabble life. The house behind him was built of island trees and thatched with the fronds of native palms, but its design mirrored the villas of Spain.

As he smiled at the foolish wisdom of Sancho Panza, Sebastian's face folded into a well worn set of wrinkles at the corners of his eyes and his mouth, disappearing into his thick white beard. Life had had been hard work all of his sixty-eight years, but it had also been fair, and his face reflected both in its wisdom and in its kindness.

He and Jada, his wife of forty-three years, had enjoyed a good life, if not an easy one. Through the window he saw her outside at her oven, stirring a pot that would be their supper that night. Her thick, black hair was streaked with grey, her waist had thickened, and her breasts had sagged over the years, but to Sebastian, her face was as beautiful as they day they had wed.

He was at the last of his coffee when Juan, the son of Lucas the fisherman came running down the path screaming and hysterical. "*Jefe! Jefe! Mi padre, los otros muertos, muertos!*"

Sebastian ran outside and seized the boy by the arms. "Juan." He shook him. "Juan. Tell me what has happened."

The boy sobbed, struggling to get the words out. "I go to the beach to take food to my father, and I find him and Mateo and Alejandro torn to pieces. Dead!" He began wailing again. Others came from their houses at the commotion.

"Where, son? Where did you see this?"

"Near the landing. By the rocks." Juan broke down in uncontrollable weeping.

Sebastian gestured to his wife Jada. "Take the boy. You men come with me." As an afterthought, he stepped into the house and took an old blunderbuss from behind the door. The men set out for the beach, fearful of what they might find.

The rosy dawn painted a grisly sight on the sand. The fishermen were sprawled on the beach, their clothing in rags, and their flesh ripped and shredded, leaving them looking more like heaps of offal in an abattoir than human beings. Sebastian handed the gun to one of his companions and leaned over Mateo's body. He traced a finger around the rough semicircle of a wound. "Shark." He spread his thumb and fingers across the bite and saw it took nearly his whole span to bridge it. "And a big one."

He crossed himself and murmured a prayer for the dead. "Go get a cart. We'll take them to the village." He shook his head slowly. "One of us will have to take a boat to Cuerpo Santo and bring back Father Beppo. These men should be buried as soon as possible."

"What was it, Sebastian?" one of the villagers said. "Was it a shark that killed these men?"

Another said, "It couldn't have been one shark did all of this. At least one of the men would have escaped. Maybe a school of sharks."

Sebastian looked out to the sea, shading his eyes with a wizened hand. "I think perhaps these men were dead before the shark had his way with them."

"If not a shark, then what killed them?"

Sebastian crossed himself again, staring at the puncture wounds on Mateo's throat. "I'm not sure I want to know."

The villagers dragged the bodies from the water. Crescent bite marks left patches of raw flesh exposed on all three corpses. Sebastian turned Mateo's head to close his eyelids and an eel slithered from the dead man's mouth. Sebastian felt his gorge rise. He regretted enjoying his breakfast so early.

Pablo and Christophe came with the cart. The mule balked at approaching the water. Perhaps it was just being stubborn, as mules will be; perhaps it smelled the blood; perhaps it sensed something else. Sebastian turned to Miguel, who stood beside him. "You and I will sail to Cuerpo Santo. I must speak to Father Beppo myself." He turned back to see the villagers lifting the remains in nets and placing them side by side in the cart. "Cover them. The rest of the village must not see them like this."

"*Jefe*, your gun." Pablo held out the blunderbuss.

Sebastian shook his head. "Put it on the cart."

He knew it would be of no use.

The sail of the little boat snapped in the wind as Miguel manned the tiller. Cuerpo Santo was four leagues to the east of Armonía, and it would take more than an hour to get there. Father Beppo sailed the distance every Sunday as he visited each of the islands to say Mass. Sebastian sat in the oarsman's seat facing the prow. Father Beppo will know what to do, Sebastian thought. Father Beppo *must* know what to do.

"Sebastian," said Miguel, "sails."

Sebastian turned his head and saw the sails of a two-masted ship coming from the horizon. Help. He would have stood in the bow of the boat and waved his arms, but he had no way of knowing who was on the ship – Spaniards? Frenchmen? Englishmen?"

"Have they seen us?" Miguel said.

Sebastian shielded his eyes with his hand. He watched the ship for a moment and replied. "Yes. Yes. They are turning this way."

"I see no flag. They're too far out. What if they're French – or pirates?"

"Then we will have other trouble. All we can do is keep moving and watch."

"By the time we can see the ship well enough; they will be so close we could never outrun them."

"If they want to catch us, they will. That is a chance we will have to take. Keep our heading to Cuerpo Santo."

The little boat plowed ahead as the larger craft angled on an intercept course. Staring into the sun, Sebastian had difficulty seeing the flag that flew from the ship's mast and wished he had a telescope. The ship would close with them before they could reach the island, and Sebastian prayed that its crew were friends and not foes.

When the ship drew within two hundred yards, Sebastian still could not determine the ship's origin. Then he saw the first puff of smoke from the deck guns. A cannonball whistled across the sailboat's path and splashed into the sea.

"A warning shot," said Miguel. "That makes no sense. We are no threat. We hailed them."

"Let down the sail. Perhaps they are simply being cautious."

Miguel did as he was told, and the sailboat bobbed in the waves.

The second shot flew across the gunwale, and Sebastian realized that striking the sail made them an easier target, exactly what the sloop wanted them to do.

"Raise the sail. Quickly."

Miguel tugged at the line but before the sail could catch the wind, a third ball struck the boat in its stern, throwing him into the water and splintering the hull. Sebastian was thrown forward and struck his head on the thwart.

As his consciousness slipped away, the voice in Sebastian's head whispered, "It is all of a piece."

On the deck of the sloop, a bearish, bearded brute lowered his spyglass. He turned to the shorter man beside him. "A direct hit, Bateaux."

"Send a boat. If either of them lives, bring him to the ship."

Sergi turned to the white-eyed crewmen and gave an order in a guttural tongue. The men turned in unison as a school of fish might wheel in the water and crossed the deck to the life boats.

"Information will be useful."

"If they can still talk."

"Even if they cannot, Varlek will still learn what we need to know."

IV

The Belladonna was running full sail, and all hands were on deck following the First Mate's instructions. Little Brio the Mate bellowed orders in a voice twice his stature as the crew scurried to capture any breath of wind to speed the ship. Near the helm, the Belladonna's captain, Diego la Mana peered through a glass beyond the ship's stern. The British gunship was not gaining, but neither was it losing ground. It was as if an invisible thread connected the ships since they had sighted each other at sunset the day before.

Diego Lo Mano, "the Hand" as he was known to the world of captains, pirates, and privateers, was one of the most successful buccaneers of the Western World, and one of the most elusive because the harder the law chased him, the more vigorously the people of the islands protected him. Diego, unlike so many of his contemporaries, was open handed with the people of the islands and generously shared his good fortune with those who treated him well, and treating him well included hiding him from the navies and the privateers who would see him hanging from a yardarm. Today was one of those days when the favor would be welcome.

"It's the Avenger and Pettigrew, sure," said Brio, the helmsman. "I'd wager my gold teeth on it."

"Too sure a bet for a sane man to take," grumbled Pike, the First Mate.

Diego lowered his glass. "It doesn't matter who's in command of that frigate. He's caught our scent and his nose won't let go of it."

"That gunboat rides low. If we can get to the shallows alongside the Exile Islands, he can't follow us without foundering."

Diego untied his thick black hair and let it fall to either side of his face. He shook his head like a wet dog and droplets of sweat flew in every direction. The ends of his mustache dripped like melting icicles. He had been hauling lines with the crew to eke every bit of speed from the sails. "By the last reading we're nearly a full day from Cuerpo Santo."

"If we're lucky, we'll make it ahead of the Avenger."

"If we were lucky, Pettigrew wouldn't have spotted us at all," Diego said, wiping his brow with his sleeve. "All we can do is run and hope we can stay out of their guns' range."

Diego cursed under his breath. Taking refuge in the harbor of Santo Cuerpo, the nearest friendly island was no bargain. If the Belladonna were discovered, The Avenger could bottle the ship in the harbor indefinitely and rake her with cannon fire should she try to leave. Worse, depending on how closely the Avenger could approach the island, Pettigrew, the Avenger's commander, could come in on the tide and fire on them at anchor, and on the village in the bargain. The Belladonna was outgunned and outmanned, so Diego had no chance but to run and pray.

On the deck of the Avenger, Captain Roland Pettigrew counted his blessings. It was sheer luck that he had sighted the Belladonna as the Avenger criss-crossed the waters south of Cuba. The larger ship should have overtaken the Belladonna by now, and it was only the sheer artistry of The Hand and his crew that kept them out of reach. He smiled. A worthy opponent made victory all the sweeter. Pettigrew had never seen the legendary pirate, but knew him well by his record of plunder and pillage from the Carolinas to the coast of Brazil. Soon, Lo Mano, he thought, we shall meet face-to-face

Pettigrew had nearly twice the sail power and twice the crew of the Belladonna should it come to a boarding fight. Let them run as hard and fast as they can, he thought. Soon enough they will exhaust themselves, and make a fatal error and the Avenger will pounce.

"He's a wizard, that one, Brackenridge," Pettigrew said to the officer beside him.

"Aye sir," said the tall whip-lean lieutenant. "A right magician he is."

"But he will find that even magic has its limits, eh?"

"Aye, sir, that he will."

Below them, the Avenger's bow split the waves, the spray glistening on the breasts of the gilded figurehead, the goddess Athena with her sword in one hand and the Aegis, crowned with the head of Medusa, in the other.

Pettigrew broke with protocol and removed his bicorn hat, exposing his heavy thatch of piebald hair that swirled dark and light like a marble cake around his crown, a look that earned him the insulting nickname Patch at Eton from the older boys until he won their deference if not their respect with his fists in and out of the boxing ring. Now he wore his parti-colored hair as a badge of distinction. He tilted his head back and closed his eyes as the wind blew through and around it cooling his scalp and soothing his soul.

Even late in the day, the heat blazed from the unforgiving sun as the men, women, and children of Armonía's neighbor island, Paz harvested their crop of sugar cane. They had begun at sunup, the men chopping with their machetes around the edge of the field and working in an ever tightening spiral, cutting the stalks as the women and children dragged them out of the way to heap them at the corners of the field.

Rosa slipped behind one of the mounds and pulled her friend Carlotta with her. "Come on," she whispered. "They won't miss us for a little while." At the age of fourteen, Rosa was just becoming a woman, her hourglass figure filling out as her baby fat melted away. Carlotta was less lucky, the same age as Rosa, it seemed that the older she got, the thicker her figure became.

"We'll get into trouble," Carlotta said.

"Nonsense. We'll just go over the hill and cool off in the spring then we'll go back to work refreshed."

Carlotta looked doubtful. "If my father finds out… ." Her voice trailed away.

Rosa grabbed her hand and tugged at her. "Oh, come on. You aren't afraid are you?"

"No, you're right. We deserve a rest. Let's go."

With a furtive look over their shoulders, the girls slipped down the path away from the cane field and followed the trail to a small grotto where a spring emptied into a shallow pool surrounded with head tall ferns. The spring was cool, and Rosa, not content with splashing water on her arms and face began undoing her dress. In a moment, its upper half hung from her waist, exposing her breasts.

"What are you doing?" Carlotta said.

"Cooling off. It feels wonderful. Why don't you try it?"

Carlotta hesitated, embarrassed at her less than comely figure. She was unbuttoning the top of her dress when she looked up and gasped at the sight of a man in filthy ragged clothing peering through the bushes. It was not surprise so much as the look of the stranger. His eyes were bluish white and his jaw was slack as if he had no mind. "Rosa," She said, pointing.

Rosa turned and saw the intruder. She cried out, covered her breasts with her forearms, and splashed across the stream toward Carlotta. The white-eyed man shambled through the brush to the edge of the spring.

The girls turned to run away and found themselves staring into the dead eyes of three more like him. Strong arms clamped around them, and wicked hands stifled their screams.

They were dragged over the bank of the spring and disappeared with their captors into the jungle.

VI

Sebastian woke in the hold of a ship, the ship with no flag, he thought, as his mind came into focus. He sat up and immediately fell back on his straw pallet as a sharp bolt of pain pierced his forehead. He remembered. They were fired upon, the boat broke up, and he fell. He carefully touched his brow and felt a crust of dried blood. Better the wound bleed its pressure out than push inward at his brain. He tried sitting up again and succeeded this time, taking shallow breaths to fight back the nausea that swept over him.

The ship was gently bobbing at anchor. He was in its brig, timbered walls and barred door. A thin vertical opening shielded on the outside in lieu of a porthole let in air but no direct sunlight. Through the bars he could see a cell at angles to either side and beyond that what looked to be a storage area lined with dozens of chests and crates all resting flat on the planking; none piled on another. Sebastian stood. His clothes were dry and salt stiff from the sea water. He put an eye to the window. Outside, the sun was shining, the sea was one shade of blue, and the sky was another. He could see no land, but his field of vision was limited.

The pain in his head dragged him back onto the straw where he closed his eyes and wanted nothing more than the room to stop spinning. In a moment, he drifted to sleep.

VII

Water splashed in Sebastian's face, waking him. A ginger bearded man in sailor's garb held a lantern over him. It was night? How long had he slept?

"*Reveillez-vous,*" the sailor said, peering into Sebastian's face.

Sebastian understood the command – he knew French well enough – but when he didn't respond immediately, the sailor repeated the command in English, then in Spanish. Sebastian raised a hand and nodded in acknowledgment.

Lightning flashed through the vestigial window and thunder boomed almost immediately. Storm waves tossed the ship, making Sebastian dizzier than before.

The sailor held the lamp higher, and Sebastian saw a scar from his hairline to his cheek that split his eyebrow. "I am Batteaux. Come with me." Sebastian tried to rise but after his second unsuccessful attempt on the rolling deck, a pair of faces swam into the lamp light that made Sebastian stiffen with distress. They were men, but not such men as he had ever seen. Their grimy faces were unshaven, their mouths were slack, and their eyes, the bluish white of cataracts, were as expressionless as those of a shark. Greasy hanks of hair framed their faces as they bent over him and lifted him to his feet by his armpits. Their unwashed bodies smelled like rotting shrimp, and in spite of himself, Sebastian gagged at the rancid odor and vomited bile down the front of his shirt.

Batteaux uttered a command in an unknown language, and one of the captors picked up the bucket and poured it down Sebastian's front. Then they hauled him dripping and coughing through the open door and past the crates and cases, now all standing open, their lids lying to the side or propped against them. Up a flight of rough hewn stairs and onto the deck where he could see the stars overhead, and in the distance, the lights of a village on the shore of one of the islands, but he could not tell which it was.

The storm rocked the boat and rain hammered the decks. Were it not for the white-eyed devils holding him, Sebastian knew that he would surely fall to the deck and roll about like a belaying pin. A wave broke over the side and he choked on a mouthful of brine.

The unkempt men half dragged, half carried him across the deck. They are like drones in a hive, Sebastian thought; mindless, simply following orders. As the neared the stern, Sebastian looked up and saw an array of figures crowding the rail, looking at him with eyes that glowed like embers, and for the first time since his capture, he felt real fear.

Sebastian was brought to what would be the Captain's cabin in an ordinary ship, under the helm in the stern. The room was lit with gimbaled lamps at the corners of the walls. Heavy red velvet curtains, dusty with age covered the windows that spread across the stern wall of the cabin. Instead of the table a captain would use to eat his supper, study his charts, and write in his log, a pair of wooden trestles supported a long wooden box. Like those in the hold, its lid was propped beside it.

As he turned to his left, Sebastian gasped. A young woman was bound by buckled leather straps, ankles and wrists, to a chair. She looked to be no more than fifteen years old, she was naked, and leeches suckled greedily at her flesh. She looked familiar. He had seen her perhaps on one of the other islands?

She did not speak. She did not squirm. Her eyes were alive, but they rolled madly in all directions as if searching in vain for her sanity. Beside her in a throne-like chair sat an aristocratic man with delicate features. He wore a ruffled shirt, green silk waistcoat, and black knee breeches over white hose and calf-high boots. His forehead was high, crowned with a shock of thick white hair that matched his brows, but his face looked youthful.

No whites showed in the aristocrat's dark eyes, and they locked gaze with Sebastian's as the man reached over the arm of the woman's chair and plucked a wriggling leech from her breast. He opened a very red mouth, and bit down on the leech, squirting his tongue with her blood. Those dreadful eyes closed then for a second as he sighed, savoring the taste, then they opened again and bored into Sebastian's soul.

"Such sweet blood," his host said in flawless Spanish. "A virgin." He dabbed at his lips with a lace edged handkerchief. "I am called Varlek." He waved a hand and one of the drones pushed a chair into the backs of Sebastian's knees and he sat, rocking backward. "Your name is Sebastian; you are the leader of your island. I suspect you have many questions for me. I have many questions for you as well, but I am a gracious host. You first. Please ask what you will."

Sebastian's jaw gaped in surprise and shock, but he managed to blurt out, "What ship is this?"

"She is named the Votrelec." He smiled, stretching his thin lips into a shallow crescent. ""In my homeland, the word means 'Invader.'"

"Why did you fire on my boat?"

Varlek shrugged. "How better to keep you from escaping?"

"Escaping? Then I am your prisoner?"

"Think of yourself as my guest for the moment."

"If I am a guest, then why was I locked in a cell?"

"I wished to talk with you. If you had awakened unrestrained and looked about you, you might have leapt over the taffrail and into the sea or otherwise harmed yourself. Once you understand certain things, you will not entertain such thoughts."

"And what of my friend Miguel?"

Varlek made a small gesture with a long white finger. The cabin door opened behind Sebastian and he heard footsteps. He turned in his seat and found himself staring into the dead white eyes of his friend.

"Now, Sebastian," Varlek said, plucking another swollen leech from the girl's body, "there are so many questions I have for you."

VIII

Diego lowered the glass from his eye. "They are gaining," he said. "Slowly, but they are gaining."

"We can do no more," said Pike. "The men are ready to fall to the deck."

"Pettigrew may catch us, but we won't make it easy."

"Aye, Captain," Pike said, "that may be, but if he does, how much fight will we have left?"

Diego's dark eyes blazed. "Enough to make Pettigrew see he's pried the lid off hell."

X

On Armonía, rain beat down on the roofs of the houses. The village men debated whether to send another boat after Sebastian and Miguel. "Surely he has had time enough by now to arrive on Cuerpo Santo and return with Father Beppo," said Christophe.

"Yes, unless Father Beppo was detained for some reason and could not come at once." Said another.

"They have been gone since morning," Christophe replied. What could detain them for so long?"

Manuel said, "Perhaps they had a problem with the boat." Manuel chose his words carefully, but Jada gasped at their perceived meaning.

"No, they are both good sailors. They will come."

"Maybe we should take another boat to Cuerpo Santo," said Raoul. "It would do no harm, and then we would know."

Several voices murmured agreement. "Very well, then," Christophe said. "When the storm ends, Raoul and I will go to Cuerpo Santo." As the others muttered in agreement, he said quietly to Pablo, "To be safe, gather everyone, men, women, and children into the chapel until we return; say it is to pray for the souls of the dead."

Pablo's eyes questioned him, but he nodded. "It will be done."

"Do you still have Sebastian's gun?"

"*Si.*"

"Keep it out of sight, but keep it close to hand."

XI

Another wave crashed over the railing of the Belladonna. knocking crewmen to the deck and washing loose items over the other side of the ship.

"Captain," Pike shouted over the howl of the storm, "we have to lower the aft sail. The wind is pushing us sideways."

"No," Diego barked back, "because that's exactly what Pettigrew will expect us to do and do it himself. If we maintain speed, we may get ahead of the worst of this and the Avenger will be caught in the brunt of the storm if they try to follow us."

"If we live to get ahead of it."

Diego ignored the comment. He crossed the deck to the helm and slapped Solieri on the shoulder. "Go below; rest a while. I'll take the wheel."

"No, Captain, I'm all right. I'll stay at my post."

"That's an order, my friend. You've been at the helm for twelve hours." Understanding Solieri's pride in his duty, he added. "Two hours. No more, and I'll expect your scrawny ass back at this wheel, or I'll come below and drag you up here."

Solieri laughed. "All due respect, Diego, that'll be the day." He went slipping across the rolling deck toward the gangway, as Diego wrapped his hands around the pegs.

"Tie me," he said to Pike, and the First Mate lashed him to the pedestal. "If the Belladonna goes to the bottom, I'm going with her."

Then like a flash of the lightning, an idea leapt full-formed in Diego's mind. "Pike," he shouted, "gather a half dozen lanterns and prepare to lower a longboat."

"Aye Captain, but for who?"

"For none of us. But it just may save our necks."

Pettigrew sat in his cabin on the Avenger, hands wrapped around a hot mug of tea. The storm wasn't the worst he'd ever seen, but it had come at a bad time in his pursuit. Three times lo Mano had escaped him on the open sea, for no want of skill or zeal on the part of his men, but often by sheer dumb luck, as if The Hand were in the Devil's own pocket.

Three times lo Mano had slipped Pettigrew's grasp because he followed orders and procedure, but this time, he was throwing the rulebook aside. On the sea, on his ship, he was Lord and Master, far from the reach of his superiors. Superiors. Pettigrew snorted. None of them was so much as his equal on the ocean, truth be told, sitting in London in their fancy uniforms and telling the real sailors what to do. This time, it was all or nothing.

A knock at his cabin door. It opened and Canty, his First Mate stepped in, shaking off the rain. "Sir, we've spotted a light."

Pettigrew rose from his chair. "A light, you say? Where?"

"Near a thousand yards off our port side. And it doesn't appear to be moving."

Pettigrew pushed his hat onto his head, frowning at the cold band across his brow, and pulled his cloak around his shoulders. There was no land for another twenty leagues by the last reading they took before the storm. It had to be a ship, and it could be none other than the Belladonna. They must have sustained damage and needed the light to make repairs. This is luck indeed, Pettigrew thought, and this time, the Lady favors me.

He stepped onto the deck and the wind blew the rain like buckshot into his face, nearly taking his hat. He climbed the steps to the poop and found Brackenridge with his eye to a glass. He took it from him and said, "Where is this light?"

"Five degrees to port, Captain," Brackenridge said, extending his arm. "If you turn just there –"

"I see it," Pettigrew said. "Helmsman, five degrees to port."

A wave crashed over the Avenger's bow. "Sir, I have to keep her head into the waves or we may capsize," the helmsman said.

"Five degrees to port, Mister Greywall. Don't make me repeat myself."

"Aye Captain. Five degrees to port."

Brackenridge drew in a long breath and kept his mouth shut. The Captain's obsession was putting them all at risk.

Soon enough, lo Mano, Pettigrew thought, as lightning flashed overhead with quick thunder at its tail. Soon enough, you'll be in my hand. He handed the glass back to Brackenridge, who peered again into the darkness. "Mister Canty, shorten sail, or we'll fly right past her."

Canty hesitated but said, "Aye, Captain," and conveyed the order to the crew.

Another brilliant burst of light. Brackenridge said, "Sir, I see it. It's not the ship, it's –"

At that moment, lightning ripped the sky again, and the explosive thunder was instant.

Brackenridge dropped the spyglass and clapped his hands to his ears. Pettigrew, eyes wide in the darkness was flash blind and half deaf from the strike, but not so deaf that he didn't hear the sharp crack of the main mast or its crash to the deck. Pinned by a spar, he felt his lungs filling with blood, and his last words were a curse, damning the Belladonna and especially her Captain.

Like all travails, the storm finally slowed and the pounding rain abated. Solieri had taken the helm again, and Diego and Pike took stock of their situation. One of the topsails was ripped, the only substantial damage from the storm. They were fortunate that they had lost none of the crew. The Avenger was nowhere to be seen on the horizon, and they were less than a day away from the Exiles.

"The ship looks to be none the worse for it," Diego said. "The gamble paid off."

"This time," said Pike, "but now there are other concerns."

"Such as?"

"We threw our food overboard to lighten the ship. We've got a hungry crew and a weary one. And we're short a longboat should we have to abandon ship."

"We'll have to put in at Cuerpo Santo, no matter the risk. We'll make it

Lightning ripped the sky again, and the explosive thunder was instant.

there by dusk and hide in the cove. So long as the Avenger doesn't show its sails, we can lay over for a day or two. Luck is on our side again."

Pike nodded but said nothing, lest his voice betray his skepticism.

XIV

Christophe hated to leave his wife and son, but the greater good must be served. The rain had lessened, but the wind still blew. As he strode toward the rocking boats, He looked to the heavens but was not sure what to pray for. Instead, he crossed himself, and wrapped the beads of his rosary around his fist. Sebastian had confided his fears to Christophe before he set sail, and Christophe could only hope that they would all live to see the sunrise. He was stepping into the little boat when he saw a lantern across the water. "Hola!" he called. Who is out there?"

"Hola!" came the reply. "It is Juan Croza and Phillipe Santos."

Christophe breathed a sigh of relief that they were men known to him. He also was relieved that they had come from the neighboring island and arrived unmolested. The boat angled to the beach and the men, dressed in farmer's garb, jumped out and pulled it onto the sand.

"What brings you here at this hour?"

"Two young women from our village, my daughter Carlotta and her friend Rosa have disappeared," Phillippe said. "We searched Paz until dark, and now we are going from island to island to try to find them. They have friends on the other islands, and we hoped they might be with one of them." His voice was at once hopeful and unconvincing.

"Have you seen them?" Juan asked, and Christophe realized that this was one of the fathers.

"No, no we have not. Have you been to the other islands?"

"Only to Luce and Speranza," Phillipe replied.

"Then you have not been to Cuerpo Santo?"

"No, not yet."

Christophe breathed a sigh of frustration. He had hoped that they might have seen Sebastian and Miguel. "No one has said they have seen anyone, but you may ask our people. You will find all of them gathered in the chapel. Three of our men died today." Sebastian crossed himself and the others followed suit.

"Three men dead? What killed them?"

"Sharks," Christophe said, knowing better and regretting the lie. "In the morning, we can search the island and see if the girls came here. If we find them we will bring them back to you."

"Thank you," said Juan.

"Where are you going now?"

"To Cuerpo Santo," Phillipe said.

"We ourselves are going to Cuerpo Santo now," Christophe said. "We will ask about them. You should go back to your people. Perhaps by now the girls have been found."

Phillipe nodded. "Yes. We will do that." He and Juan put their shoulders to their boat and pushed it off the shore.

"I pray you find your daughter safe," Raoul said to Juan, "and her friend as well. *Vaya con Dios.*"

"And to you," said Phillippe as the waves pulled their boat into the deep water.

"Have we been cursed?" asked Raoul. "So many things wrong at once from so many directions."

Christophe stared out at the darkness and made a decision. "If Sebastian's suspicion is correct, all of our troubles may sprout from the same poisoned stalk. Let us sail and I will share what he told me."

XV

The drones threw Sebastian back into his cell. He landed roughly on the straw pallet and rolled into the wall, jarring his aching head. The storm was abating, and the Votrelec no longer heaved in the waves. Votrelec, he thought, Invader. Invading his island, his home.

He had tried to resist Varlek's questioning, but as he stared into the bottomless wells of those eyes, he felt his will eroding, like sand under his feet sucked away by an outgoing wave.

"And how many people on Paz?" he asked, "and how many are men? Women? Children? And what defenses do you have on your islands?" The questioning went on for what seemed hours, until Varlek had wrung every detail of the Exiles from Sebastian. Then the white-eyed thralls, Miguel among them, half-led, half carried Sebastian back to the hold and to his cell.

Sebastian had turned to face Miguel and was about to beg his friend for help, but the vacant look on his friend's face made him realize that he might as well beg a tree or a stone. Miguel belonged to Varlek now. The door slammed shut, and the key turned in the lock, leaving Sebastian alone in the darkness.

But not for long.

Through the bars he saw dancing red embers like fireflies moving from the other end of the hold. As they neared him, he saw they were moving in pairs, eyes glowing dully in the blackness. They hovered outside his cell, then they began to push through the bars. Sebastian cowered in the corner of the cell. Lightning flashed dimly through the window slit, and printed an image from hell in his eyes. Taloned hands groped through the spaces trying to reach him. Faces, many faces pressing inward. Faces with long sharp teeth and devil eyes, faces that snarled and mewled like tortured cats in frustration that he was out of their reach.

One of them began whispering, "Sebastian, Sebastian," and the others joined in, not in unison, but in a cascade of competing voices like a sepulchral waterfall. He shut his eyes and pressed his thumbs into his ears and realized the whispers came from inside his own head. He began whimpering, but soon his sobs became moans, and then one long shriek of terror. They were calling him to them, to the bars where their fangs could reach his flesh. He felt himself rise and on legs that were no longer his to command, he began to stagger across his cell.

"*Dost*!" The voice was like a whip crack, and so strong even in his stoppered ears, that it threw Sebastian sideways onto the deck. He opened his eyes and saw Varlek standing outside his cell. The vampire's face glowed like rippling silver moonlight. He seized one of the creatures by the hair and another by his nape and flung them aside like toys. The others fell away from the bars, cowering, faces to the floor to escape his wrath.

"This man is not for you," Varlek snarled, his voice cutting like a cleaver. "Away from him." The creatures crawled, on their hands and knees and slithered on their bellies, averting their gaze from their master's angry countenance. Beyond Varlek, in the darkened hold, Sebastian heard the heavy thump of wood as some climbed into crates and pulled the lids over them to hide their frightened faces. Not crates, Sebastian thought, call them what they are, coffins.

Varlek turned his shining face toward Sebastian. It hung like a paper lantern just outside the bars. "My apologies. They will not trouble you again. Sometimes in their hunger and enthusiasm, my Anointed forget their place. I need you alive, and I can't have them driving you mad."

"Need me? For what? I've told you all you asked." Sebastian croaked, his voice strained from screaming.

"The Exiles – an apropos name – look to be just the sort of place I need as a refuge. And I could take the islands one by one, as I have so many for so long, but the islands alone are not sufficient. I need people to maintain them."

"Slaves, you mean," Sebastian spat. "Or cattle?"

"Cattle?"

"I know what you are. Like the *brujas* of Anaga in Tenerife, or the *Guaxa*. You live on human blood."

"You are wise beyond your years, Sebastian." Every time Varlek spoke his name, it plucked some string deep in his being and resonated with seductive power. "You think that you know the meaning of persecution. Your forebears fled Torquemada's madness, but you have lived in peace for generations. I, on the other hand, have fled for many lifetimes, pursued by peasants and kings, never truly at rest. I have sailed on this ship for decades always running, never at peace. I weary of the chase."

The words slithered into Sebastian's ears, hypnotic in their delivery. He felt them having their way with them. I must resist, he thought. Pain. Pain will distract me. Sebastian bit down on his tongue and tasted the coppery blood.

"If I could make my demesne on your islands, I would be away from those who would destroy me, and should they come, be able to defend myself and thus survive.

"You could help me. And in so doing, help yourself and your family, and your people. I would need a regent, and you are already the *jefe* of Armonía. You are known and respected. The people will hear your voice. You could negotiate terms of surrender, and perhaps avoid violence to them. You will find I can be a benign ruler, and the rewards will be great."

"You want me to be your servant? To betray my people?"

"No, not betrayal, Sebastian, salvation."

"Will you turn us all into those white-eyed devils?"

"The *trúdovi*? No, they are useful but they have no minds of their own. After so many years of forcing my will or buying it as I have with Batteaux and the other men, I want devotion."

"You want to be a god."

"In other ages, I would already be a god. But the arms of the Church are long and its hand intolerant. If I cannot be a god, it will be enough to be a king."

Sebastian's mind raced. He wanted no part of Varlek's scheme, but he also realized that if he were dead, he could help no one, and Varlek would continue killing until he found a willing ally. Sebastian shuddered at the thought of a wholesale attack by those creatures.

Dead, he could do nothing; alive, he might find a way to subvert the evil plan. "And if I accept?"

"I will begin by placing you in more suitable quarters." Varlek pointedly turned his head toward the hold behind him, suggesting what would happen should Sebastian refuse. "I will return before dawn for your decision."

"There is no need to return," Sebastian said. "I accept."

Varlek smiled broadly, showing his fangs, and as he did, a clap of thunder like the voice of Doom shook the timbers of the Votrelec, putting the Devil's Amen to the bargain.

XVI

As the storm raged outside Armonia's chapel, rosary beads clicked and prayers were murmured not only for the three dead fishermen but now for the safe return of Sebastian and Miguel, Christophe and Raoul.

"They should have never gone to Cuerpo Santo, Pedro." Adrián said, the furrows of his brow deepened with concern. He crossed himself.

"They could never have anticipated this storm," Pedro replied, peering out into the rain swept darkness watching for he did not know what, and keeping his hand near the blunderbuss hidden behind the stoup at the chapel's entrance. So much water, he thought, listening to the rain, and so little of it sanctified. "We can only hope that they landed before it caught up with them."

"The women want to clean and dress the bodies for burial." It was their custom that the dead be buried within twenty-four hours.

"Tell them that Father Beppo cannot come until the storm passes. We cannot have proper funerals without him to say Mass."

Adrián nodded and stepped away; leaving Pedro at his watch to think about the horrors the women would see when they finally performed their duty. Out there, something out there in the dark, beyond the glow of the votive candles waiting, watching, but he knew not what. Pedro dipped his fingers into the holy water and traced a cross on his forehead. Dawn and its reassuring light could not come quickly enough.

XVII

The storm was abating. Christophe and Raoul were able to raise their sail once again, after hours at the oarlocks steering their boat into the heaving waves to prevent capsizing. Both were exhausted and drenched in sweat and brine, but mercifully alive. Raoul sat at the tiller, as Christophe consulted his compass by the flickering light of their lamp. "Twenty degrees to starboard should put us on course."

"Just so." Raoul pulled the tiller and the prow of the boat swung to. "The storm blew us far off course, but we will find our way."

"We must."

XVIII

On the Avenger, Lieutenant Brackenridge sat in the wardroom at table staring at the empty chair at the table's head. In a few moments, the officers would file in and sit at the table and stare at the chair as he now did. He could almost see the dead Captain, leaning back in the chair puffing at his pipe, giving a lynx-eyed stare as each of his fellows made their reports and accounted for their actions.

The Captain was dead, and Brackenridge had to assume command. His ears still rang from the crack of thunder that followed the lightning bolt. The storm that snapped their mast had wound down, but now new crises presented themselves. Decisions had to be made, and as senior officer, Brackenridge had to make them, but protocol and common sense dictated that he make them only after consulting the other officers now under his command.

A knock at the cabin door. Brackenridge nodded to his seat. The men were respectfully silent before Pettigrew's empty chair.

Brackenridge broke the silence."We are faced with a multiple dilemma, gentlemen, and I ask your advice. First things first. What is the state of the ship?"

"The worst damage was the main mast," Blake, the Sailing Master said. "Keaton will have the chandlers at it at first light. He has the section to replace the damaged one on hand. We could still sail in the meantime, but at a much slower pace. We would do badly in combat until the repairs are made. With luck, it'll be done by the end of day."

"Casualties?"

"We lost two by my count," said Clark, the surgeon. He paused and nodded toward the empty chair. "Including the Captain."

"Who is the other man?" Brackenridge asked.

"Willoughby, one of the gunnery team."

"Two more, Sykes and McPherson, are missing; likely overboard in the storm." Blake added.

"And injuries?"

"One broken arm and the rest cuts and bruises," Clark said. "Our losses were small in numbers, but –" His voice trailed off as he turned his palms upward.

No one spoke for a moment. Then Brackenridge continued. "It is regrettable, but the death of the Captain forces me to assume command. If any of you has any misgiving about that, I want to hear about it here and now, not have doubt scuttling around the ship like a wharf rat."

After a contemplative silence, Lieutenant Berks raised a hand. "Permission to speak freely, sir."

"Granted. What is it, Mister Berks?"

"It is arguable that Captain Pettigrew placed us in this jeopardy by pursuing his obsession with capturing the Belladonna and Diego lo Mano, and caution to the wind. Do you intend to continue this pursuit?"

Brackenridge leaned back in his chair. He stuffed his pipe and lit it from a candle, taking the time to draw a few puffs from it. He already knew the answer but needed time to consider how best to present it. "In a word, yes." Muttering broke out around the table. Brackenridge rapped his knuckles on the table and the murmurs ceased. "Gentlemen. Please allow me to clarify my answer. We almost had the Belladonna, and had not the storm interfered, we would have overtaken her."

"But surely she is long gone by now," Berks said.

"Not necessarily. She threw her food overboard to lighten the ship. She will need to re-provision at her first opportunity. Brackenridge unrolled a chart on the table and the officers leaned in to peer at it. "This is our approximate position." Brackenridge put the tip of his index finger on the map. To the southeast lies a small group of islands called the Exiles. They house a colony of Spanish Catholics; farmers, fishermen, craftsmen. Those islands are the nearest source of food and water in more than fifty leagues. I'm thinking that the Belladonna will put in at one of them. If we are underway by nightfall, we may catch them yet."

Again, murmurs around the table, but the tone was changing. "I would add that the storm damaged the Avenger; perhaps it damaged the Belladonna as well. If so, their delay may match our own, and we have lost little advantage. Does that answer your question satisfactorily, Mister Berks?"

Berks' head bobbed in an affirmative nod. "Indeed, sir."

"Very good. I would also add that my continued pursuit of the Belladonna at this moment is not merely a gesture of devotion to the memory of our Captain; it is also a matter of duty, and I will exercise all discretion in the performance of that duty. Are you men with me?"

Nods and ayes all around the table.

"Very good." Brackenridge gestured to his steward who brought a tray with bottle and glasses. Rounds were poured. "And now gentlemen, let us drink a toast to our late Captain. May his body sleep in the bed of the sea to which he devoted his life, and may his soul rest in the bosom of Our Lord."

The whiskey burned all the way down, and Brackenridge immediately sobered to the responsibility that had fallen across his shoulders.

XIX

Despite Varlek's promise, Sebastian was not moved from his cell that night. The moans and wails of the vampires in the hold carried on until dawn, when the noise ceased as if a door had shut. Every bone in Sebastian's body ached, and his eyes burned from fatigue. In the absence of the vampires' caterwauling, Sebastian was finally able to think. From what he knew of vampires, all of them, including Varlek would be at rest until nightfall.

His situation was monstrous; either betray his people and lead them into bondage or be thrown to the horde of vampires just outside his cell. Alive he still might be able to thwart Varlek's scheme in some way; he didn't know how that could be done, but at least he could try. Dead, he could do nothing. He closed his aching eyes and prayed fervently until he ran out of words to say.

Father Beppo worked, stripped to the waist, hoeing the little garden he kept behind Cuerpo Santo's church. He was a short, powerful man with a close cropped beard that blended into a fringe of grey hair at his temples. His broad shoulders glistened with sweat in the morning sun. His was a simple life, a far cry from his past when he served at the Vatican, before his banishment to the Exiles for his skepticism and dissent. He did not miss the fine vestments, the luxurious apartment, or the grand meals, but he did miss the Library. Learning was his passion, and here, there seemed to be little to learn.

He tended his garden as he tended his flock, methodically, carefully, cultivating their faith as he did his beans, peppers, and plantains. To allow one weed a foothold led to its multiplication, and the loss of the whole crop. Consistency and discipline were the mainstays of his ministry.

The church was anything but grand in the material sense, built of native wood on the outside and thatched with palm fronds, with the inside fitted with benches, a pulpit, and an altar crafted from the planks of one of the ships that brought the refugees to the New World. It was built in detail along the traditional plan on a smaller scale in defiance of the Vatican from narthex to apse. The crucifix that hung behind the altar and the Stations of the Cross were lovingly hand carved by Rodrigo Panza, the leader of the exiles a century before.

Beppo admired their faith, their determination, and courage, not unlike his own, challenging authority with which they disagreed. In the end, the refugees of Torquemada's madness were not excommunicated, as threatened, but from that day they became neglected stepchildren of the Church.

Yet, the flock exhibited a faith that rivaled those in the Vatican, forced to flee, the proclaimed heretics clung all the more strongly to their religion, and devoted themselves to it. Beppo had been in the grand cathedrals of Rome with their gold, silver, and stained glass, and found them no more comfortable than Cuerpo Santo's simple House of God. In fact the simple church offered a warmth the magnificent structures, for all their grandeur, could never achieve.

At the sound of footsteps behind him, Father Beppo turned to see two men approaching, men he knew as Christophe and Raoul from Armonia.

His face shifted from a greeting smile to a look of concern when he saw the grim expressions on the visitors' faces.

"My sons, what is wrong?"

"Terrible news, *Padre*," Christophe said. "Three men dead on Armonia," He removed his hat and clutched it to his chest. "And two missing."

"How did these men die?"

"We found three on the beach. They were eaten by sharks. Sebastian and Miguel sailed here last night to ask you to come, but we fear they were lost in the storm."

"Sebastian de la Vega? Your island's *jefe*?"

"And two young women," added Raoul.

"Young women?"

"Yes, Father, two girls from Paz, missing from their island as of yesterday."

Father Beppo brushed the dirt from his hands and crossed himself. "I will come to Armonia at once."

"We have a boat ready, Father," Raoul said. "We can leave as soon as you are ready."

"I must gather a few things from the church, but I won't be long."

Christophe bowed his head and gazed at the flowering herbs in the priest's little garden. Father Beppo's hoe lay where he had set it down. How easily an ordinary day can be turned on its head, Christophe thought, and its simple joys be replaced by terrible responsibility.

Moments later, Father Beppo emerged in his cassock and broad-brimmed hat. He carried a leather valise in one hand, and a stoneware bottle in the other. "I must leave word where I'm going. Come with me." The village on Cuerpo Santo was almost double the size of Armonia's, a larger cluster of houses with the church as its center and a marketplace between the village and the docks.

As they passed through the market, the villagers greeted Father Beppo. He raised a hand in blessing as he moved among them, wearing a reassuring smile despite his sad duty as Christophe and Raoul followed him. He approached a stall where a tall, heavily muscled man was cutting fish with a long, curved knife. He was Cataldo, the *jefe* of Cuerpo Santo. He looked up as the trio approached and nodded a respectful greeting to the priest. His wife Nina worked beside him.

"Good day, Father." His voice rumbled like an empty barrel rolled down a flight of stairs.

"And a good day to you, Cataldo. These men are from Armonia, they have suffered a death, and I must go to the island."

Nina crossed herself. Cataldo grunted and looked over the priest's shoulder to Christophe and Raoul. "Your kin?"

Christophe said, "In a community so close knit, we all are kin."

Cataldo nodded."May we help in any way?"

Raoul broke in. "Two of our village sailed here last night to fetch Father Beppo. They have not arrived, and we fear they were caught in the storm. Could you send boats out to look for them?"

"The fishermen are at sea now. If your men are alive between here and Armonia, they will be found."

"But if they were blown off course –"

Cataldo sighed and set down his knife. "When the boats come back this evening, if there has been no sign of them, we will all go out to search. There is little more that we can do."

"Thank you, my son," said Father Beppo, and to the others, "Now, let us go."

"And, Cataldo," said Christophe, "have two young women come to the island in the last day?"

Cataldo's eyes narrowed. "Not to my knowledge. Who are they?"

"Daughters of Paz named Rosa and Carlotta. They too are missing."

"I will enquire."

"As they walked away, Nina said, "You should have asked who died and how."

Cataldo slapped a large sea bass onto the cutting block. He picked up his knife and deftly slit the fish longways. "If they wanted us to know, they would have told us. We will learn soon enough." He shook out the entrails, swept them from the table into a chum bucket, and began scraping its silvery scales. "The less I hear about trouble, the less I have to do about it."

"But –"

Cataldo's look silenced her, and she went back to cleaning fish.

XXI

Raoul and Christophe and Father Beppo went to the dock and climbed into the boat. The priest settled in the gunwale. They cast off and Christophe waited until Cuerpo Santo was a short line of green above the blue water before he turned to Beppo and said, "Father, there is more I must tell you."

The priest nodded knowingly. "I've been waiting. I knew there would be more. Death is terrible, but what I saw in your faces reaches far beyond that."

"Before he left for Cuerpo Santo, Sebastian told me of his suspicions. The dead, Lucas, Alejandro, and Mateo, were savaged by sharks, but the men were perhaps already dead when they were bitten."

"By what cause?"

"The bodies bore other bite marks, not the ragged half moon of a shark, but two small holes in the flesh."

"On all three men?"

Christophe nodded. "And in several places on each."

"A bite but no flesh torn?" Father Beppo gazed out to sea, a silent prayer on his lips.

"Father, what do you know of vampires?"

Beppo was careful with his reply because he knew full well that the Holy Father, Benedict XIV, declared that vampires were "fallacious fictions of human fantasy." But Beppo had lived too long and in too many places to dismiss anything out of hand, a skepticism that saw him removed from his post in the Vatican and sent from one outpost to another before being sent to minister to the Exiles. "Only what legend tells us, the *Guaxa*, the Anaga witches, and the hell-hound, the *Dip*. They are undead, perpetuating their foul existence by drinking the blood of living souls. Does Sebastian believe that is what killed the men?"

"He fears so, and that is why he came for you himself. He did not want to panic the village. And that is why I waited until now to tell you. I was afraid that someone might overhear."

"And the missing girls, does Sebastian think they are a part of this?"

"Sebastian did not know of them before he left to find you."

"It may be all of a piece," Father Beppo said, wiping his brow. "We can only pray that it is not. Sebastian was right to not panic the villagers. I will see the dead for myself, and then we will decide what may be done." He eyed the angle of the sun breaking through the clouds. "We have much daylight left, and from what I know of the vampire, he cannot move about in the sunlight, so we have sufficient time to discern what to do. It may not be a vampire at all. But if it is, you were right to gather the people in the chapel. God's House may be the only safe haven they have."

Christophe opened his mouth to reply, but stopped short at the sight of the priest, crucifix pressed against his bowed forehead, silently mouthing a fervent prayer.

XXII

The storm had blown the Belladonna further off course than Diego had thought, and Cuerpo Santo came into view in the late afternoon. "Bear west," he told Solieri. "Circle the island. I don't want the villagers to see us in case Pettigrew arrives and demands information from them. We'll put in at the cove on the south side of the island then I can take some men through the jungle to the village."

Solieri grinned. "Aye, Captain. That's a plan. When you threw the supplies overboard, I hope you spared the rum. We'll all need a drink when this voyage is done."

"You know me well enough; I'd pitch rum overboard last thing before the booty."

Solieri laughed. "And for that we love and serve you."

The sun broke through the clouds and the winds were fair. The Belladonna and her crew had been lucky once again, but that didn't keep Diego from posting a watch in the crow's nest to keep an eye behind them. Pettigrew was not one to give up, easily or otherwise.

XXIII

The sun was at its zenith when Father Beppo stepped onto the sands of Armonia. "It bodes well," the priest said. "Man at his full stature."

"I do not understand, Father," said Christophe.

"The riddle of the Sphinx," Beppo said. "What walks on four legs in the morning, two at noon, and three at sunset? The answer: Man, who crawls on all fours as an infant, stands erect on two in his prime, and limps on a staff in his twilight years. Like Man, the day is at its height, and we are full strength and girded to act with the day's remains."

Christophe and Raoul led Father Beppo to a hut at the village edge. Inside, planks on trestles held the three corpses. Beppo waved away the flies and drew away the blanket that covered them. A simple test would tell him what he needed to know.

The bodies were ghastly, their wounds gaping crescents of raw flesh, like waning red moons. He turned Mateo's head to the side and saw the two small punctures under his chin. He poured a few drops of holy water from his bottle onto the wound, and the liquid began to roil and bubble, turning to steam in seconds.

"What does it mean, Father?" Raoul asked.

"It means that Sebastian's fears are confirmed, and that we must act quickly. Gather the men of the village. Have them prepare to sail to the other islands."

XXIV

Cataldo was at the dock when the first of the fishing boats returned. As the crew tied up at the pilings, Cataldo approached them. "Why are you in so early?"

Santino, the owner of the boat waved him closer. "We found this in the water." The little man held up a section of a small craft, splintered planks pegged to a beam."

"Did you find survivors?"

Santino shook his head. "No, *jefe*, no survivors, nor any dead either."

Cataldo's jaw tightened. "Do the other captains know?"

"We have seen no one else from the island."

"You will have to go back, find the other boats and all join in the search."

"And, Cataldo, there is one thing more. We saw a ship in the distance to the north. Two masts. Too far away for us to see a flag. Perhaps they picked up the men from the boat."

"Let us hope so. That may be our only hope of finding them alive. We will sail out to meet them and inquire." He swept the offal from his butcher's block into a wooden bucket with his knife and set it aside. He held out his hands while Nina poured a bucket of water over them, rinsing off the blood and the scales.

XXV

Brackenridge sat at the table in the captain's cabin. Pettigrew's chair stood empty. He could not yet bring himself to sit in it. Beside the

Christophe and Raoul led Father Beppo to a hut at the village edge.

Bible on the table lay the possessions Clark, the surgeon, had removed from the Captain's pockets: his pipe and a drawstring leather tobacco pouch, a purse with three gold Sovereigns and an assortment of small coins from various currencies, and a heavy silver pocket watch. Brackenridge opened the case and saw the smashed crystal and hands stopped at the moment Pettigrew fell.

These things would be placed in Pettigrew's chest with his other belongings and stored away until they reached a port where they could find a ship to carry them home to the Captain's family. He would write a letter to Pettigrew's widow, expressing his condolences, but what words could he summon to stanch her tears knowing that he died for an obsession?

A knock at the door. It was Clark. "The men are gathered, William."

Brackenridge rose from his chair. To this point, command seemed a nebulous thing, but this, his first official act in the role of Captain brought the reality into sharp focus. When the old man went into the sea, the Avenger and her crew lay squarely across his shoulders. He picked up his Bible and left the cabin.

Brackenridge had waited until the mast was repaired before gathering the crew to hold Pettigrew's funeral. The men crowded the deck. Emotions were mixed. Some were mournful, some indifferent, and the few who disliked the Captain at least had the decency to refrain from smiling. As Berks had once put it, "You needn't worship a man to obey his orders."

The sun shone on the calm waters, a complete contrast to the peril of the night before. On the starboard side of the ship, a ramp with the Union Jack over it had been set to deliver the bodies into the sea. Pettigrew and Willoughby lay side by side, sewn into their bedsheets, each weighted with a cannon ball, equal in Death.

Brackenridge removed his bicorn hat, and the crew followed suit. He opened his Bible to the place marked by a black ribbon and began to read.

"'Man that is born of a woman is of few days and full of trouble. He cometh forth like a flower, and is cut down: he fleeth also as a shadow, and continueth not.'" He raised his head and looked into the faces all around him. "We here honor men who sailed with us into battle, men who stood shoulder to shoulder with us against sword and storm, and who have fallen into death in that pursuit, gunner's mate Thomas Willoughby, carpenter Martin Sykes, seaman Colin McPherson, and Captain Roland Pettigrew."

He unfolded a piece of paper from the back of the Bible and read the Prayer for the Dead.

"'We therefore commit his Body to the Deep, to be turned into Corruption, looking for the resurrection of the Body when the Sea shall give up her dead, and the life of the world to come, through our Lord Jesus Christ; who at his coming shall change our vile Body, that it may be like his glorious Body, according to the mighty working, whereby he is able to subdue all things to himself.'"

A drum roll sounded across the deck. Hands put Willoughby's body on the ramp under the flag and tilted it so the body slid from below the flag and splashed into the water below. Sykes and McPherson followed. Pettigrew was last, and as his body sank into the sea, one of the men began the Lord's Prayer, and those who knew it joined in. At the Amen, Brackenridge replaced his hat and said, "Back to your stations. We have a pirate to catch."

XXVI

Cataldo stood in the prow of the boat as it approached the two-masted ship, glass to his eye. He had been born on Cuerpo Santo and had never left the island, but as a boy he studied the ships that put in at the port for trade or supplies. This one flew the French flag and sported the name Votrelec in tarnished brass letters on its bow. Cataldo knew French but did not recognize the word. He began to wonder if the ship were a pirate vessel under a false flag. The gun ports were closed, but could open at any moment. It was a risk to sail closer, but he could do no less.

The Votrelec seemed to be lying at anchor, mainsails furled, bobbing in the gentle swells. There was little activity on deck. A few crewmen moved back and forth, and the ones he could see were a scurvy looking lot. On the bridge, Cataldo saw a telescope pointed at him. He set down the spyglass and waved a broad swath of white linen to indicate peaceful intent. In a moment, the gesture was returned, but Cataldo was still wary. "Sail to them head on," he told his helmsman. He wanted to make the boat as narrow a target as possible. As they neared the ship, Cataldo watched the gun ports lest they suddenly open.

As they came alongside the Votrelec, three men came to the rail, a short man with sandy hair and spectacles, a huge burly man, bald and bearded, and a lean man wearing a seaman's cap; the man with the telescope. No one else was in sight. Odd, thought Cataldo. I would think more would appear if only from curiosity. When they reached hailing distance,

Cataldo cupped his hands around his mouth and called in the best French he could muster, "Ahoy, Votrelec. We are from the island of Cuerpo Santo. We have lost a boat with two men aboard. Have you seen them?"

The man who had watched Cataldo's approach said, "I am Batteaux, the First Mate. This," he pointed to the bearded giant beside him, "is Sergi our helmsman, and Pescu, our purser. We have one of your men, Sebastian de la Vega. His companion, alas, has died."

"Is de la Vega well?"

"He is." Batteaux turned and spoke to Pescu, who left the rail. In a moment, he returned with Sebastian at his side.

"Sebastian," Cataldo called, "We have come to return you to Armonia. "

"There is no need," Sebastian replied in Spanish. "The Votrelec will deliver me to the island. The Captain is most gracious."

"We can spare you the trouble," Cataldo said to Batteaux.

"It is no trouble at all," he answered. "We need stores, and Sebastian tells us that Armonia can supply us. We will be there by nightfall."

Cataldo's jaw clenched. Sebastian had snatched an opportunity for trade from under him. Great thanks for the trouble they took to find him. "Very well; as you wish." Cataldo said to his helmsman, "Turn us around. We're going back." There was still the matter of the missing girls.

From the deck of the Votrelec, Sebastian watched Cataldo's boat sail away, wishing he were on it. Batteaux spoke in the strange guttural language to two of the *trúdovi* who rose from their crouches below the rail and took Sebastian by his arms.

"You will go back to your cell for now," Batteaux said. "Varlek will want to speak with you later."

"But you said you would bring me back to Armonia."

"Yes," said Batteaux, "by nightfall. Not before."

Sebastian took a long last look over his shoulder at the disappearing sail of Cataldo's boat as the *trúdovi* roughly dragged him across the deck and down into the dark hold.

XXVII

Christophe and Raoul sailed into the harbor cove of Esperanza, the smallest of the Exile Islands. Boats that should have been at sea fishing bobbed at the pilings. No one was in sight. They moored their sailboat and hesitated to step onto the dock. They heard the sounds of birds and of monkeys in the trees, but no sounds of people. "This is not good," Raoul said, looking around fearfully.

Christophe took the boathook from the stern, and Raoul a machete from beneath the seat. Without speaking, the pair climbed from the boat and started toward the village. The wide path led through waist high ferns with palm trees towering overhead. Near the village, they found an overturned wheelbarrow, its load of cocoanuts spilled on the ground. Christophe walked around it studying the earth.

"What are you looking for?" Raoul said.

"Blood. But I see none. Whoever was hauling this load dropped it and ran." He raised his head and looked ahead of them. The village was another hundred yards, around a bend in the path. "No smoke, no noise, no people."

Christophe stood and turned full around, listening and searching the undergrowth for eyes. He strode in the direction of the village. Raoul clutched the handle of the machete a little tighter, and followed behind him. In a moment, the tops of the houses were visible through the palms, a dozen or so grouped around the village chapel.

The closer they came, the sound of birds increased. When they rounded the bend in the path, the first thing they saw was the mass of gulls, hopping, pecking, and flapping wings at each other, fighting over scraps of raw flesh.

The second thing they saw was what the birds were worrying over, the corpses of men and women, their clothing in tatters, and their skin in shreds. The bodies were covered with the scavenging birds. Christophe picked up a stone and threw it at the nearest corpse. The birds flapped away with angry cries and retreated a few feet, little black eyes watching for their chance to swoop in again and resume their grisly feast.

The body was a woman, short, stout, her dark hair in a long braid curled around the ruin of her face. Her jaw had been torn away and hung to the side, her tongue lolling and her perfect white teeth forming an arch at the roof of her mouth. The birds had pecked out her eyes, and her sockets stared at them, dark and empty.

"Dead how long, do you think?" said Raoul, looking away from the gory corpse.

Her dress had been shredded, the exposed breast bearing a fan of slashes as if a taloned hand had seized it and squeezed, claws hooked in the skin and meeting where a gobbet of flesh had been torn away. A similar patch had been ripped from her left thigh, but what had killed her was a gash in her throat, blood dried in a black patch on the front of her peasant blouse. Beside her, a dog lay, disemboweled.

As they chased the birds from one corpse to another, each presented a new horror; limbs torn off and cast aside, claw marks ending in ribbons of skin, but one feature was uniform: the expressions of unbridled terror and pain on every face. Nowhere did Christophe see the puncture wounds at any throat. Fourteen dead that they could see; where were the others, and how many dead? Esperanza had at least thirty people. If some survived, where were they?

Beside all of the men and some of the women lay their weapons; machetes, axes, and shovels. Near one, Christophe saw a dismembered hand. He turned it over with the boat hook then speared it with the barb on the end. He raised it to his face and studied it closely. The curled fingers ended in nails that curved into vicious claws. Dried blood and tatters of skin were lodged under these nails.

Raoul stared over his shoulder at the hand. "That is no human hand." He began babbling, words tumbling out. "It is the hand of a beast, of a demon, *mano del Diablo*, his eyes rolling in terror.

Christophe swung his arm and slapped Raoul across the side of his face with the back of his hand. Raoul cowered from the blow but came to his senses.

"Stop it. If we break down, we are of no use to anyone." He swung the boathook to put the hand in Raoul's face. "This is no demon, no spirit. It is flesh, and it is dead." He tipped back his head and shouted, "Ho! Anyone! Anyone! Answer me!"

The only sound was the chatter of monkeys and the cawing of gulls.

Christophe shouted again, and Raoul said, "Please, Christophe, let us leave this place."

"Yes, we must go next to Caridad. I pray we will not find another scene like this."

There were dead to be buried on Esperanza and survivors, if any, to be sought, but Christophe told himself that the dead must wait. It was the living who must first be served. The people of Caridad were more likely to be alive, their numbers second only to Cuerpo Santo's. They must be warned, and quickly. Then back to Armonia to tell Father Beppo what they had found.

"To the boat," he told Raoul. He took a last look around the village. By the time they disappeared around the bend in the path, the gulls had covered the corpses again with a writhing, screeching feathery blanket.

XXVIII

The men of the village gathered in the barn where the corpses of the fishermen lay. Father Beppo waited to address them apart from the women and children. They stood in a group, hats in their hands out of respect for the priest and the dead. Beppo took a long breath and finally spoke.

"My sons, a great evil has come among us. We must be as one to overcome it. Some of you have seen what has happened to Mateo, Alejandro, and Lucas. For those of you who have not –" He waved away the buzzing flies and pulled the cover from the corpses. Some of the men gasped, others silently crossed themselves. All had seen death before, but never so ghastly.

"They did not die from the bite of a shark." Beppo turned Mataeo's head to reveal the twin punctures at his throat. "They died from the bite of the *vampiro*." At the sound of the word, murmuring broke out among the villagers.

"What do we do against such an evil?" one of the men said. "How do we protect our children, our wives, ourselves?"

"We fight," a tall man said fiercely. "We fight to defend our home."

"If it is the great evil the Holy Father says it is, how can simple men like us fight it?"

"We fight the *vampiro* with this." The priest held his crucifix over his head for all to see. "The demon fears the holy sign. The power of the Lord will protect you."

"Protect us, yes," said the tall man. "But how do we drive it away?"

"We will find a way. In the meantime, we must work together to keep everyone safe. Gather your families. You will all sail to Cuerpo Santo. We will take refuge in the church. The evil cannot cross its threshold. Also, the fiend walks only by night. We have many hours before the sun sets. There will be time.

"You men with boats, take the children and the women first, then return for the men." He bowed his head and offered a prayer for the dead and a prayer for the living.

As the men dispersed, one of them said, "But, *Padre*, what of Mataeo, Lucas, and Alejandro? They must be buried."

"I will see to it that they are properly cared for, my son."

The man nodded and joined the others on their way to the cove. Father

Beppo turned back to the men on the table. He would wait until the villagers were gone to burn the bodies. Otherwise, they would rise and join the creature that killed them.

He laid a finger beside the marks on Mataeo's throat then laid the finger beside a bite on the fisherman's leg, then on his forearm. He did the same with Lucas and Alejandro then carefully covered the bodies again. Many bites, he thought, many different spans between the fangs.

Many vampires.

R aoul sat on the thwart, head in his hands while Christophe manned the tiller. Their next stop was Caridad, close by Esperanza. Christophe was sickened and frightened by what they had seen, but unlike Raoul, he was galvanized by it and spurred to action. Christophe's mind leapt from one horrific answer to another. The people of Esperanza were not killed by vampires, but they were savaged by something no less evil. What nagged at him was the fact that there were no corpses of children. Where had they gone?

I n his cell, Sebastian heard a commotion. He rose from his pallet and peered through the bars across the gloomy hold. The *trúdovi* were carrying children down the stairs. The captives wailed as they were dragged kicking and struggling between the coffins. The cells on either side of Sebastian's were opened, and the children pushed roughly inside them. The doors clanged shut, and the *trúdovi* left the new prisoners, some sobbing and wailing in the half-darkness, others silently staring at a land far beyond the bars of the brig.

"¿*Señor* de la Vega, *Eres tu?*"

Sebastian pressed his face to the bars to look to the side of his cell. He saw a dark haired girl of about fourteen years, looking plaintively from her cell, hands wrapped around the bars and face framed by them. Tears streaked her face, her hair was a tangle, and her chest heaved with sobs. "Yes, child. I am Sebastian de la Vega," he replied. "Who are you?"

She gulped, swallowing a sob. "I am Marla Sandoval. I live on Esperanza." Her voice shook with emotion. Like so many adults, Sebastian knew her father and mother but never paid attention to their children. "These horrible men came to the island. They took us onto a boat and brought us to this ship. What do they want of us?"

"I do not know, Marla," Sebastian lied, for he knew all too well Varlek's plans for the young and innocent. He remembered the girl with the leeches and shuddered. "I too am a prisoner."

"They took you from your island?"

"No, I was on a boat and they took me from the sea. But what of your parents?"

"I haven't seen them. Some of us were on the beach digging clams when the boats arrived with the big bearded man. We saw the men with the white eyes, and tried to run, but it was too late. They took us onto a boat and soon more came with others tied together as we were and brought us to this ship. What will happen to us?"

Sebastian said sadly, "Child, I do not know."

Footsteps at the other end of the hold. Batteaux came with two of the *trúdovi*. When the children saw them, they began screaming. Batteaux took the ring of iron keys from his belt and unlocked Sebastian's cell. The thralls entered and took him by the arms.

"Where are you taking me?" Sebastian demanded as the *trúdovi* dragged him through the doorway.

Batteaux smiled. "Varlek keeps his word. You'll learn that before too long. He promised you new quarters, and you will have them now. Besides we need your cell for captives." As they took him away, Marla thrust her arms through the bars, reaching for him, and Batteaux put his hand through the bars against her chest and shoved her away. "Get back in there."

Sebastian tried to break free to intervene, but the thralls' grip was unyielding. As they dragged him across the hold, Marla's cries were lost among the wails of the other captured children.

He was taken on deck and by his reckoning at least three hours of daylight remained before the coffins would open and those things, the vampires, would emerge again, and three hours before Varlek would wake. Varlek had said that he would deliver Sebastian to Armonia by nightfall and if he kept his word, Sebastian would at least have a chance to sound a warning, even if it meant his death.

The new quarters were a cramped cabin below decks in the bow, originally designed for storage, no windows, no hatch, only a heavy oaken door on strap hinges. It was lit by a gimbaled lamp high on one wall. A bunk stood opposite the door alongside a crockery jug of water and a slop bucket. On the bed lay a set of clothes, breeches, a shirt, and shoes. One of Batteaux's crewmen came in with a plate of bread and cheese and a small carafe.

"You'll wash up and dress now," Batteaux said. "Varlek wants you presentable."

"Presentable? For what?"

"He doesn't tell me his plans, my friend, only what he expects of me."

"But–"

Batteaux closed the door and turned the key in the lock.

Sebastian was alone.

Like any prisoner in a new cell, he took the measure of the place. Twelve cubits wide, four deep, and seven high at the apex of the sloping ceiling. The boards were pegged together as tight as a clam shell, walls, floor and ceiling. No chance of escape. The bunk was likewise solidly built. He couldn't dismantle it without an axe or a heavy hammer. And as soon as Batteaux and his men heard the pounding, they would be in the room in an instant anyway. No chance of using a leg from the bunk as a club, or breaking a sharply pointed piece away to use as a stabbing weapon. He was not by nature a violent man, but if there was nothing he could do to harm Varlek, there was nothing wanted more than a club to smash Batteaux's face and pound his skull to bloody gravel.

The jug held brackish water for him to wash himself. He stripped out of his tattered clothing and poured the water over his head, letting it cascade over him from his head to his toes. Then he dried himself with his own clothing as best he could, the fabric stiff and roughened by the brine. He put on the new clothing, garb borrowed from some sailor. It was a little loose on his old man's frame, but the fit was good enough. Compared to his sea-roughened clothes, the shirt and breeches felt like silk.

The bread was hard and had mold along the crust, but not so much as the cheese. Yet, Sebastian was so hungry that he ate every crumb of the food. The water was clear and fresh; it had probably come from a rain barrel on the deck.

After eating, Sebastian lay on the bunk. He stared at the gently swaying lamp overhead, and its rhythm lulled him into fitful dreams. In Varlek's cabin, Sebastian was untying the ropes that held the young girl to the chair as the leeches crawled over her flesh. His fingers struggled with the rock-like sailors' knots that held her shins to the legs when a heavy hand clamped onto his shoulder.

He turned his head to see Miguel, staring at him with blank eyes. The hand on his shoulder tightened, Miguel's nails, now claws, digging into muscle and sinew. Sebastian tried with both hands to pry those taloned fingers from his shoulder, but to no avail.

The grip tightened and as Miguel's fingers met his thumb around Sebastian's collarbone and yanked him to his feet, Sebastian screamed.

He woke, eyes wide, sitting upright on the bunk, a rivulet of icy sweat trickling down his back. He lay down and stared at the swaying lamp, but sleep would not come again.

XXXI

The last boat was ready to leave from Armonia. Father Beppo gathered the acoutrements of the Mass from the chapel's altar, the chalice and paten for communion, and the candlesticks, and was packing his bag when Juan came into the chapel. He took his hat from his head and held it with both hands. "*Padre*, the boat is ready to sail. You must come now. The sun will soon set."

Beppo put his hand out to take the wooden crucifix, carved generations ago by one of the early refugees and stopped. No, he thought, let the demon come with his minions and let them look on the naked face of the Savior. He bowed his head for a brief prayer, picked up his bag, and left the chapel.

"This way, *Padre*," Juan said, but Father Beppo had one last thing to do. "Go on ahead," he told the man. "I will be there shortly."

Beppo followed the path to the barn where the corpses were laid. He held his crucifix before him and said, "*In nomine Patris et Filii et Spiritus Sancti.*" One of the corpses groaned, all three began writhing as if in discomfort. He was correct. There was only one thing he could do. He took the lamp from the wall and poured its oil on the corpses. The sun would set at any moment; he had no time to lose.

He struck flint to steel and the oil caught, but not before the sun fell below the horizon's rim, and one of the bodies, Mataeo's corpse sat up, engulfed in flames. It tried to climb from the table but its ravaged limbs could not hold its weight, and it fell to the floor, catching the straw ablaze. Behind him, Alejandro and Lucas, both ablaze, rose and staggered toward the doorway. Alejandro fell on his face, but Lucas bobbed and jerked, flailing stiff-armed in the middle of the fire, beating at his flaming face

Sheets of fire climbed the walls, and soon the entire barn was burning. Father Beppo backed away, crucifix in front of his face, and the Mataeo-thing came crawling after him on its working knee and elbow. Then the roof fell in, and a beam landed across the vampire's back, pinning it to the floor. It howled in rage and frustration as it watched its prey disappear into the darkening jungle.

Beppo ran for the mooring, not because he was afraid, but because he understood the need to put as much distance between the island and his charges as he could and as quickly as possible.

XXXII

Sebastian stood on the deck of the Votrelec, flanked by two of the *trúdovi*, who held his arms in an iron grip. In the gathering twilight, he saw the silhouette of Armonia's landscape, the small mountain, an extinct volcano rising to catch the last light of day as they sailed toward it. When they were inside the bay, he would be taken ashore by Batteaux and some of his crew to meet with the islanders and offer them their lives in exchange for perpetual servitude.

His meeting with Varlek had been brief. At sundown, he was brought to the vampire's cabin where Varlek lounged in his throne-like chair. The girl with the leeches was gone, but the chair with its leather restraints stood by as a reminder. Varlek sat with one leg over his chair's upholstered arm swirling a snifter of red dark liquid in his delicate palm. He inhaled its aroma as if it were vintage brandy, and sighed deeply.

"I could have killed you or turned you," he said, his speech seeming to echo in the close cabin like it would in a canyon or a cave. Sebastian realized that Varlek spoke aloud, but at the same time he heard it with his ears, the words rang inside his skull. "Do you know why I did not?"

Without waiting for an answer, the vampire said, "I have lived for centuries, long enough to know human potential when I see it. You are no simple peasant, you are intelligent. You are a leader of men. You are someone who can make my takeover of the Exiles much simpler and much less costly to both parties.

"I could swoop of a night and take the islands by force, but I am a reasoning person; to do so would take many lives, the lives of your people, people who would become my subjects."

"Slaves, you mean," Sebastian snarled. "Or perhaps cattle for you to feed on at your leisure."

Batteaux drew back his fist to strike Sebastian, but Varlek held up a restraining hand. "Let him have his say. I need to know what Sebastian thinks before I send him on so critical a mission." Varlek's eyes bored into Sebastian's. "You think I want to simply enslave your people? I will make them wealthy, allow them to live in luxury they never dreamt before. I can be benign if I am satisfied. A beloved Lord."

"And what do expect of me, *Lord* Varlek?" Sebastian's voice dripped with sarcasm.

"I expect you to use your position and the trust of your people to persuade them to submit quietly and willingly."

"There are too many who will not go like lambs to the slaughter."

Varlek smiled. "Some may resist, but not many after they see what befalls those who oppose my will."

"And if I oppose your will?"

Varlek signaled Batteaux with a wave of his forefinger. Batteaux left the cabin and returned with two of the *trúdovi,* holding a struggling Marla between them. They shoved her roughly into the empty chair. In a moment, her arms and legs were strapped to it, and she sat, quivering with fear at this new monster.

The vampire reached under his chair and held out a crystal bowl of leeches, swimming about in murky water. He reached in and plucked one from the bowl. He held it in front of his face, studying it as it squirmed in his grip. Batteaux ripped the girl's dress to the waist, exposing her budding breasts. Varlek dangled the wriggling leech over Marla's bosom and tipped his head toward Sebastian, looking at him from the tops of his pale grey eyes.

"Sometimes, Sebastian, one's own pain is far less persuasive than another's, would you not agree?"

Sebastian swallowed visibly and said. "All right, Varlek, let the child go, and I will not resist you."

Varlek laughed. "I admire your nerve Sebastian, to make demands of me." He dropped the leech into the bowl. "She will remain in that chair for the time being; until I see that you are a man of your word. We sail now for Armonia, where you will make your case to your people. I hope you are persuasive."

And now, Sebastian stood on the deck of the Votrelec watching the silhouette of the island as it seemed to rise from the sea. He had the words in his head, but did not know whether he could bring himself to speak them. Then he thought of the child, Marla, and realized that he must.

XXXIII

Cataldo ground his teeth. Cuerpo Santo was being invaded by refugees from the other islands, boatload after boatload pouring into the harbor. It was all the doing of that meddling priest Beppo. And by what right, Cataldo thought, did he stir up the islanders and send them all for him to manage? Beppo's collar gave him spiritual authority, but not secular authority. Did the scriptures not say "render unto Caesar?" The priest had told them simply, "Leave your island, go to Cuerpo Santo, and they did as they were told. And where was the good *Padre* to answer for all this?

As he watched, another boat, crowded with anxious faces, most of them women and children, came gliding toward the dock. Cataldo strode angrily toward the boat that had just unloaded its passengers. The men on board were casting off, pushing away from the dock.

"Wait. Stop," Cataldo shouted, but the men ignored him.

Cataldo grabbed a rope tied to a piling and threw it like a riata. Its loop caught a mooring cleat on the bow of the boat. Before the man in the bow could remove it, Cataldo wrapped it around a piling and tied it off. Straining every muscle in his body, he pulled the line taut and hand over hand began to drag the boat back to the dock.

"Please," the man at the tiller begged. "We have to go back for the rest of our people." Cataldo recognized the man as Raphael Garza from Paz.

"And bring them here? Not until you tell me why you do this," Cataldo demanded. "Why do you bring these people to Cuerpo Santo?"

"Danger," Garza said. He looked from side to side and came to the bow of the boat and said in a lower voice, "Father Beppo, he says we are in danger. He says we must gather here, in the church. It is the only safe place for us."

"Danger from what?" Cataldo said.

"From this." A voice behind him. Cataldo turned and saw Christophe holding a gnarled hand on the barb of a boathook. He had just stepped from the boat tying up at the mooring. "Raoul and I went to Esperanza, and we found no one alive. They had been murdered, and we found this hand by the bodies. It is not human."

Cataldo pinched one of the fingers, ran the tip of his forefinger along the edge of the talon. It was as sharp as his boning knife. "This – they came from the sea?"

"It seems so."

The ship with the strange name, Cataldo thought. The ship that rescued Sebastian. "And the attack on Esperanza, that is why the priest told everyone to come here?"

"That is one reason, but there are others far worse." Christophe leaned in to speak softly. "Father Beppo speaks of vampires."

"What?"

"The undead." Christophe recounted the deaths of the fishermen and what Father Beppo discovered about them when he came to Armonia, and his call to warn the other islands.

"Vampires." Cataldo spat. "I don't believe in such things."

"Then believe in this." Christophe raised the hand between their faces. "There is danger and death, whatever the cause may be. That is why the islanders come for refuge."

Cataldo looked over his shoulder. While he was talking with Christophe, the boat he had stopped was slipping away from the dock and into the twilit harbor.

"When Beppo arrives, we will talk."

"Until he does, you should make use of the time to prepare."

"Prepare for what?"

"For the evil that is coming."

XXXIV

The Votrelec sailed into Armonia's cove as the last light faded. Torches marked the dock but there were few boats bobbing at the mooring. A longboat was lowered, and Sebastian, Batteaux, two human crewmen and a dozen *trúdovi* climbed down the ladder and took their places. Sebastian and Batteaux sat in the bow while the *trúdovi* pulled at the oars. The humans carried cutlasses and muskets, the *trúdovi's* weapons, swords and

"We found this hand by the bodies. It is not human."

axes, lay by their feet. Sebastian was relieved that Miguel was not with them. At least Miguel's wife and sons would not have to see the white-eyed obscenity that he had become. Sebastian looked behind him and saw that the Votrelec's gun ports were open. Perhaps Varlek was not so confident as he seemed.

"So few boats. Do your people fish at night?" Batteaux asked.

"They fish with the tide," Sebastian said. "The sea is its own clock."

Batteaux grunted. "If they return too soon, they may meet with tragedy." He jerked his head toward the ship with its guns at the ready.

"So may we if they open fire."

"A risk we run."

The closer they came, the more apparent it became to Sebastian that the island was deserted. Every boat was gone from the mooring, although it was not unusual for the islanders to cast their nets at night. Through the trees he saw the flickering lights of torches in the village, but saw no movement. The boat touched the dock and Batteaux and his men stepped off first, muskets at the ready. The *trúdovi* climbed from the longboat, two of them holding Sebastian by his arms.

Batteaux turned to him. "Do your friends go to bed early, Sebastian? No one has come to greet us. You keep no watchmen?"

"It has not been necessary," Sebastian lied, knowing that the dock was routinely guarded against thieves and pirates.

Batteaux told his men, "Advance carefully. I don't know what's happening here, but it may be a trap." He turned to Sebastian, "You beside me. Your people will be less likely to fire on us if they see you in the lead."

The visitors moved with slow caution. The path from the dock to the village was hard-packed sand and shells, which made it difficult to see tracks. Batteaux's men swept the shadowed undergrowth with wary eyes, while behind them the *trúdovi* plodded along, blank eyes staring at nothing.

The smell of wood smoke hung in the air. The usual torches stood along the paths through the village, but no lights shone in the houses. No fires burned in the hearths. Every house they entered told the same story. Kitchens were left in the midst of cooking supper, wooden pestles and spoons in bowls of plantains and rice, fish scaled and boned, a cut of lamb in an iron pot with vegetables, waiting for the cooking fire. A child's toy left on the floor. An open book. A torn shirt in the midst of being mended. People lived in these houses, but none was at home. It seemed a great hand had plucked them from their places in the midst of life.

The benches in the chapel were likewise empty. The crucifix stood on the altar in defiance of the invaders. Batteaux raised his musket. A flash and boom, and the crucifix exploded into shards. The party gathered in the village square.

One of the sailors rounded the corner of a house. "A building, probably a barn has burned. We found bones inside, three men."

Sebastian's mind raced. Mataeo, Lucas and Alejandro, destroyed before they could join Varlek's minions.

Batteaux ground his fist in his palm. Unless the Armonians were hiding in a cave, the island was deserted. Varlek would not be pleased. "How did you do it?" he asked Sebastian.

"Do what?"

"Warn your people. Did some signal pass between you and that ape Cataldo today?" Batteaux eyed him coldly.

Sebastian shook his head. "No, I swear it."

"No matter. Varlek will have the truth from you." He spoke a word to the *trúdovi*, who roughly seized Sebastian. "Which house is yours?"

Batteaux lifted a torch from its stanchion. "This one?" he pointed with the torch. "Or perhaps this one?" The look on Sebastian's face gave away the answer. Batteaux was about to throw the torch through the open doorway but stopped. "I shouldn't destroy anything here, even your house. Varlek may decide that he likes it well enough to make it his home. Besides," he said with a sardonic grin, "anything we destroy we'd likely have to build again sooner or later." He dropped the torch on the ground. "Back to the boat."

XXXV

It was full dark when the boat brought Father Beppo to Cuerpo Santo. Cataldo was waiting. Priest or not, he would answer for the tumult he had caused.

"Now, *Padre*," Cataldo said, seizing the priest by the shoulders. "Tell me what is going on. In detail."

Beppo raised his face to stare fiercely into Cataldo's eyes. "The Devil has come to the Exiles."

"Talk sense," Cataldo demanded, a little too loudly, shaking the priest, and attracting the attention of some of the men, who immediately surrounded him. "That man is a priest," one of them said. "He is saving us all. Take your hands off him."

"I must go to the church."

"Not until you explain yourself."

"Let go of him!"

Cataldo's eyes swept the group, armed with axes, hammers, and knives. The fear in their eyes made him realize his peril. He let go of Beppo and stepped back. "You are right," he said quietly. *"Mis disculpas."*

"Come with me," said Father Beppo, who broke through the gaggle of men and strode down the dock. Cataldo glared at the priest's protectors as if to say, "I'll deal with you later," and fell in step behind him. He heard the feet of the islanders fall in behind him and realized that the power of the Church reached far beyond his own in the eyes of these men.

XXXVI

The vampire wore a long dark coat with red frogs over a crimson silk shirt that made his face look even more pallid than it had. Perhaps he hasn't yet fed, thought Sebastian. Marla sat in the chair beside him. Unlike the girl Sebastian had seen before, she didn't have the vacant look in her eyes he'd seen on the other girl. Her eyes bulged with terror over a gagged mouth.

Varlek's face was impassive, but his voice dripped with cold fury. "No one? Not one soul on the island?" He sat upright in his chair, hands gripping the arms.

Batteaux cringed under Varlek's tone, recognizing the danger that lay beneath it. "No, one, Master; we searched the island. All were gone."

Varlek fixed his gaze on Sebastian. "You. How did you warn them?"

Sebastian fought a tremor in his voice. "I did nothing, gave no warning."

The vampire's face began to writhe. The corners of his eyes tilted upward, the mouth broadened until it seemed to wrap halfway around his head. The ears extended to sharp points, and the chin thrust outward like the blade of a plow. His fingers elongated and curved into wicked claws.

Varlek rose from his chair. He walked slowly around Sebastian, tasting his aura. He stopped face on and took the man's head in his hands, thumbs on his cheekbones, their talons perilously close to Sebastian's eyes. Sebastian wanted to scream, to bolt and run away, to leap over the rail and dive into the sea to escape the monster that stood before him, but he was frozen in place by the monster's will.

He felt Varlek's mind slither through his own, touching his thoughts, his hopes, his singular fear. He shuddered in spite of himself as Varlek read him, as easily as he had read Cervantes the morning before. The vampire stared into Sebastian's eyes for a long moment, then released his grip. "He has done nothing. Something else must have raised an alarm." Varlek's features relaxed. He sprawled in his chair. "Take him away." He waved a dismissive hand. The *trúdovi* led Sebastian out of the cabin. "And the girl as well."

Two of Batteaux's men carried Marla, still bound to the chair through the door behind Sebastian, leaving Batteaux alone with the vampire.

"This changes much," Varlek said, stroking his chin. "Someone on those islands knows what I and my brood are, and if he does, he knows what can destroy me. He must be found."

"But you also have the *trúdovi* to guard you by day while you sleep, and my crew to see that no one boards the Votrelec. No matter what these peasants know, they cannot touch you."

Varlek smiled. "Batteaux, if I believed that, I would not be on this ship, ever moving from place to place. Knowledge is power, and whoever has that knowledge is a threat to me. The old saying is that Satan's cleverest trick is to make people believe that he does not exist. A single believer is a threat to me, and he must be silenced, although he has disrupted my plan already. I want no further interference. Sebastian recognized the signs, but he is well read. Someone else knows, and must be stopped."

Batteaux nodded and backed out of the room. On deck, he closed the door and leaned against it, his head spinning. He had seen Varlek's transformation before, but he would never become accustomed to the sight.

XXXVII

The church was brightly lit with torches. Hundreds of islanders were packed into a space designed for sixty at best. People sat on the benches and sat on the floor. They filled the dais behind the pulpit. Infants lay in their mothers' arms, and small children straddled their fathers' necks. A loud murmur came from the group as they talked among themselves, but it ceased at once at the sight of Father Beppo striding through the crowd that parted before him as he made his way to the pulpit.

He was still wearing his robe, the hood back, revealing a taut face beneath his horseshoe of grey hair. Cataldo stood at the rear of the church, arms folded, waiting for explanation while the rest waited only for solace from their priest.

Father Beppo turned his palms upward in supplication and looked to the heavens as he recited a prayer and crossed himself to a collective amen from the flock.

"My children," he said, his voice filling the room. "The Devil has come to our islands."

Gasps and sobs rippled through the congregation.

"But we have the shield of faith to protect us from his evil." His gaze swept the faces of the flock. "The Scriptures say, 'Yea, though I walk through the Valley of the Shadow of Death, I will fear no evil.'"

"What evil?" Cataldo's voice boomed over the heads of the islanders. "What is this great evil that makes you all cower in here like frightened children? Tell us, *Padre*, what must we fear that you cause such a panic?"

"We must not fear, Cataldo," the priest said, pointing a finger at him. "We must have faith and let that faith deliver us from fear. But we must also fight. We must do as the apostle says and pick up the shield of faith and the sword of righteousness to protect and defend ourselves with the Savior's help."

"Defend ourselves against what?" Cataldo demanded.

"Vampires."

Cataldo snorted in derision. People in the flock began to wail and to moan. Others began murmuring. The sound swelled and Father Beppo raised his hands. "Please, be quiet," he shouted over the din. "You must hear me."

"Silence." Cataldo's voice boomed like a cannon. "Tell us, *Padre*, what proof do you offer?"

Christophe leapt onto the dais. "The proof lies dead on Esperanza! Men, women slaughtered by fiends like this!" He held the dead hand aloft for all to see. "Who here is from the island?" No one raised a hand. "Raoul and I found no one alive, and the children missing."

"I went to Armonia to bury the dead fishermen," said the priest, "but when the sun set, their bodies rose. I had to burn them with fire to purify them."

"But vampires are creature of the night, Father," one of the men said. "I was at Esperanza this morning, and all was well. If they were all dead before sunset, Death must have visited in the daylight."

"If not vampires, then something every bit as evil, something that does not fear the light," said another. "Men?"

"Perhaps men once, but men no more," the priest answered. "Thralls to the vampires, undead, men without souls."

Cataldo spoke up. "So, which is it, *Padre*? Vampires, or something else?"

"Perhaps both."

Again the buzz of voices swept through the crowd.

"So what must we do?"

"We must rely on the power of Faith and the Lord to deliver us, but we must also strive to save ourselves. The Lord helps those who help themselves."

"How? What can we do?"

"We must fortify this place. The vampire cannot enter holy ground, but perhaps something else can."

"But not until daylight," said Christophe. "We must remain inside the church until dawn. If we go outside, we may be taken."

"So for now," said Beppo, "we wait." He looked to the crucifix hanging over the altar. "And we pray."

XXXVIII

Varlek stood beside the helm of the Votrelec as it bobbed at anchor. Below, longboats were carrying *trúdovi* to the island to secure it. Perhaps events worked out well enough after all. He would occupy Armonia without loss and from its vantage point, be able to attack and defend until he controlled the Exiles entirely. But he had lost the element of surprise, which was an annoyance at the least. If the islanders knew what he was, they would be ready for him, based on the limits of their knowledge. The tales of the *Dip* and the *Guaxa* were fables that traded more on superstition than fact. Sebastian's knowledge was limited, but someone else's hand was in play, someone more knowledgeable.

Batteaux joined him. "Will you spend the night on the island?" The vampires' resting places, empty for the moment, would be moved ashore once suitable places were ready. Varlek had three coffins with his native soil in all; two were already on the island.

Varlek thought it over. "No. I will spend one more night on the Votrelec, to be safe."

"As you wish."

Batteaux climbed down the ladder into the waiting longboat. Varlek watched as *trúdovi* pulled the oars with Batteaux in the prow. There was no love in the man for Varlek, nor true devotion, but he would serve at Varlek's pleasure so long as the vampire wanted.

As the *trúdovi* pulled the oars, Batteaux looked back at the ship with despair. Varlek had tricked him into his service, hiring him as first mate before he realized what Varlek was and what he expected him to do. One night in Marseille, the newly employed first mate woke to a knock at the door of his cottage. He opened the door to find Varlek on his doorstep.

Batteaux was surprised to see him. Varlek strode boldly into Francine's room, wrapped the screaming girl in his cloak and disappeared into the night.

Batteaux's wife Emma, whose heart was weak, died of the shock.

The next night, Batteaux sat in his cottage staring at Emma's body, washed and dressed by the neighbor women, ready to be sewn in a sheet and buried in the churchyard. He was most of the way through a bottle of brandy and thinking the thoughts of a man who has suffered unspeakable tragedy at the hands of another, when a knock sounded at the door.

A young boy stood on his doorstep holding an envelope. Batteaux opened it to find a note from Varlek penned in a beautiful, practiced hand, summoning him to the Votrelec.

He went to the ship with a pistol hidden in his coat. He was brought into Varlek's presence in his cabin for the first time. The fiend, wearing his human face, sat in a throne-like chair, flanked by two *trúdovi*. Behind him, Batteaux saw a large, long box on trestles. Varlek smiled benignly. "You desire to kill me," he said. "I understand that, and you may try if you wish."

Batteaux stood frozen by the vampire's gaze. He opened his mouth to speak, but no words came.

"I assure you, that your daughter is safe and well, and she will remain so as long as you serve me faithfully. You have seen my true face now, Batteaux, and I needed surety that you would neither flee nor reveal me."

He gestured to the *trúdovi*, who raised the lid. Francine lay, eyes closed in what Batteaux realized was a broad, silk lined coffin. Her hands were folded demurely across her breast, and her expression was one of peace and security. He stepped forward to the coffin, but the *trúdovi* blocked his path. Varlek spoke a word Battaeux did not understand, and the minions stepped aside.

Batteaux gripped the sides of the coffin and stared at his daughter. He was suddenly aware of Varlek's presence beside him. The vampire had glided, noiseless as a shadow across the cabin. "Touch her if you like," he said. "Assure yourself that she lives."

Batteaux then leaned over her and put a fearful finger to her throat. He felt her pulse flutter, as light as a moth.

"What have you—"

"She sleeps, my friend. And she will sleep unharmed until such time as you have finished your service to me."

"And if I serve you? You will release her?"

"That, friend Batteaux, depends strictly on your devotion – to her and to me."

Batteaux drew the pistol from his pocket and offered it on his palm to Varlek.

"You brought this to kill me?"

"Yes."

Varlek cocked the hammer, and Batteaux thought the vampire was going to kill him with his own weapon. Instead, Varlek turned the pistol to his own breast and pulled the trigger. A flash, a sharp snap, and the sound of breaking glass as the ball broke a pane of glass in the window behind him.

Batteaux started back, staring at Varlek, who smiled and undid the strings of his ruffled shirt. Batteaux stared at a puckered hole in Varlek's chest ringed with the grey of gunpowder. A single drop of blood so dark it looked almost black oozed at the lip of the hole. Varlek took it on the tip of his finger and touched it to his tongue. He handed the pistol back to Batteaux. "Don't blame yourself, friend Batteaux. There was nothing you could have done but cause your own death. You have my word Francine will neither be harmed nor violated so long as you obey. And you will quickly learn that my yes means yes and my no means no. Come at sunrise. We will sail on the evening tide." Varlek turned away, and Batteaux was shown from the cabin.

He walked with numb steps down the gangplank and across the fogbound dock, turning toward home without even thinking, realizing for the first time in his life what it meant to be damned.

+++

Varlek watched the longboat disappear into the darkness. Batteaux would be just as happy to be elsewhere this night. He left the deck and went into his cabin. His closed coffin was large, too large for a single occupant, but not out of vanity. Varlek raised the lid, and the light of the lamps shone inside on the figure of a beautiful young woman, clad in a gossamer gown of pale blue. Her lustrous hair framed a face like a cameo, porcelain white with delicate features. He took a hank of her hair and held it to his lips. The vampire touched her face and closed the lid.

Batteaux had neither love nor devotion for Varlek, but so long as he held Francine suspended between life and death, Batteaux could refuse him nothing. The sun would rise soon, and Varlek would sleep. Soon enough, he thought. My plans will bear fruit soon enough.

"Sergi," Varlek said, barely audible, but in a moment, Batteaux's next in command appeared at the vampire's side. The Russian was an inch taller than Varlek himself, bald to his ears but sporting a thick shaggy beard and an angry red scar across his forehead that made his face look as if someone had pulled his head from his neck, turned it upside down, and stuck it back on again. "Yes, Captain?"

"Weigh anchor."

"Yes, Captain."

Silence filled the church; the islanders huddled in the nave. Some slept fitfully, mostly the children, feeling a false sense of security in their parents' embrace. Many of the adults sat wide eyed, clutching crucifixes their hands nervously clicking rosary beads.

Father Beppo called the leaders of the islands to his quarters to discuss in detail what steps could be taken to ensure the safety of their people. The men sat or stood as space permitted and listened as the priest recounted events on Armonia. "The Holy Father says that vampires are a fantasy of men, but sometimes Satan can make fantasy come alive to suit his purpose and to defy the Lord, and I believe that has happened here."

"And we are powerful enough to combat the Devil himself?" Cataldo said.

"Do not the Scriptures tell us, "'resist the Devil and he will flee from you?'"

"But if what you say is true, there are many devils. How can we resist them all?"

"With faith and the strength of our hands."

"The legends say they fear the light of day," said one of the older men, "or so my grandfather told us when we were children."

"And they cannot bear the sight of the holy cross," said another.

"But how can they be killed?"

"A stake through the heart," said Father Beppo. "That has always been tradition. That and exposing them to sunlight. They are harmed by silver and by Holy Water. I know of no other ways."

"We have little silver," said Pedro, "but we have much water. Can it be made holy?"

Father Beppo nodded. "Yes, it can, but it will take time."

"But what of those invaders who are not vampires? The ones who attack by day?" Christophe said. He held up the severed *trúdovi* hand.

Cataldo stabbed a finger at it. "That hand is flesh and bone. If it can be cut it can be stopped. Nothing walks without legs."

Several of the men murmured assent.

"Then I will deal with the vampires," said Beppo. "You can deal with this other, whatever it is. Tonight we keep watch. Tomorrow, in daylight, we fortify the church, all the while keeping watch for invaders from the sea. This ship you saw, Cataldo, how large was it?"

"Two masts. It should hold a hundred twenty men. But there is another peril. The ship's sides are lined with gun ports. They can sail into the harbor and fire their cannon into the village and perhaps even into the church if they wish. We have only two cannon on Cuerpo Santo, not enough to hold them back."

"It will have to do. I will bless the guns in the morning, and we can only hope that God will guide their aim." The priest crossed himself and said, "Let us pray."

XL

The Belladonna rounded the spit of land that curved like a protective arm around the cove to the eastern side of Cuerpo Santo. The ship had sailed east for part of the day, then circled back to arrive at the island just before dawn. Diego had traded with the islanders of the Exiles in the past, and they were happy for the business, but they still regarded the pirates with a wary eye. Because of the religious nature of the islanders, the Exiles offered none of the pleasures that sailors on leave would want; no taverns, no whores, no gambling dens, and for that reason, most ships passed them by. And so long as the Belladonna's crew behaved, their gold was welcome if not themselves.

"Odd," Brio said. "I would think we'd see fishermen on a clear night like this."

"Just as well," Diego replied. "We don't want anyone announcing our presence if the Avenger's moored at the other side of the island."

The Belladonna could not be seen by the Avenger unless the ship sailed into the cove because of the trees and undergrowth on the arm. If they lay quiet and dark, they would not be easily found. The shadows were slipping from black to violet as the sun prepared to rise to paint the cliffs that rose a hundred feet from the water. There was no mooring, so the ship had to lie at anchor while Diego, Brio, and a half dozen of the crew rowed to the base of the cliffs, to a spot hidden behind heavy brush where a set of handholds were carved into the rock for climbing. On the Belladonna, gun crews sat at the ready, just in case.

They pulled the boat ashore and dragged it behind the tall ferns. The climb would be risky in the near dark, but Diego had little choice. The notches were cut deep into the granite and the climb was not as difficult as it might have been. The sultry, humid air was like breathing steam, and all of the men were sweating and short of breath when they reached the plateau at the top.

The plateau was dense with trees and jungle ferns, and the mosquitoes were relentless. Their shrill whine deviled the pirates' ears as they picked their way through the grey light. The sweet fragrance of tropical flowers mingled with Night birds called to each other, and in the distance, they heard the coughing snarl of a jaguar.

Diego found the path through the jungle well cleared and simple to follow, but the trek was slow going. The men had to drag their toes, so as to not stumble in the darkness over roots as thick as a forearm that criss-crossed the path. Their boots would protect them from scorpions, but the silky webs strung tree to tree by spiders as big as a man's palm were a nuisance. No native spiders had venom potent enough to kill, but the bites were painful. In the lead, Diego brushed more than one web from his face as they went, the sticky tendrils clinging to his hair and beard.

It would take more than an hour to reach the town and the harbor and there Diego would seek out Cataldo, the island's chief to negotiate for supplies. The quicker they were provisioned and on their way, the better. The Avenger couldn't be too far away, and may be searching the Exiles at that moment. The path wound down the steep slope from the plateau and through a break in the trees Diego saw stars around a slim crescent moon. Little light for our journey, he thought, but likewise, little light for our pursuers.

The trail wound down the mountainside and Diego saw a farmhouse nestled in a small, protected nook. Cattle lowed in the thatched barn. He smelled smoke from a wood fire, but something else as well, burnt flesh. He signaled his men with a wave of his hand, and they quietly crept to the house. Diego sidled to a window and peered inside.

The farmhouse was empty, and the smoke was coming from the remains of the cook fire in the hearth. Diego found the door ajar and slipped inside. The only light was the glow from the rough stone hearth, but in its light, he could see that the house was empty. An iron kettle hung from the crane over the fire, and in the room, the acrid stench was stronger.

He used a coal rake to catch the handle of the kettle and swing it away from the fireplace. Its bottom glowed a dull red. He then lit a piece of kindling from the coals and used its flame to see into the pot. In it were desiccated turnips, yams, and a blackened chunk of meat; a stew that had been left to boil down and burn. Why? And where the people who lived here?

"This is not right, Diego," Brio said, looking this way and that as if something would spring on them at any moment from the shadows.

"I agree. Something strange is happening. We'll find out what it is when we reach the town." He poured a ewer of water into the kettle and steam drifted up the flue. "Let us go."

XLI

The Avenger lay at anchor within sight of Esperanza, the westernmost of the Exiles, waiting for first light to go ashore and search the island for any trace of lo Mano and his crew. The watch had nothing to report for hours, Brackenridge sat in the captain's chair, swirling a glass of brandy in his palm and staring at nothing. He seemed to have inherited Pettigrew's obsession along with his command. He felt an obligation to his late captain's memory to catch the Hand and either bring him to justice or bring justice to him at the point of a sword, the muzzle of a gun, or the end of a rope.

Brackenridge now understood how easily one could be caught up in another's quest until it eclipsed all else. If he failed, his commander had died for naught, and the indelible stain of failure would be his and tarnish his name and career for the rest of his days.

So for the past day and a half, the Avenger criss-crossed the ocean, all eyes on watch for lo Mano's sails. Brackenridge was certain now that the Hand had taken refuge on one of the Exiles. He resolved to search every island and woe to those who gave him shelter. The islands were Spanish, and at the moment, a fragile truce existed between King George and Charles the Third. Brackenridge would not deign to upset it, but piracy was a crime that knew neither flag nor nation. The Hand knew no allegiance; he stole from all crowns, and Charles should be as glad to be rid of him as anyone.

Still the risk existed. In the morning, his men would land on Esperanza. If they failed to find the pirates there, he would move west from island to island until he found them. To land on a Spanish territory with armed men and mount an operation could constitute an act of war. To justify it to the diplomats and the Royal Navy, he must have results. He must deliver the Hand to the Admiralty, lo Mano, or his corpse.

He tipped the glass and felt the brandy burn the back of his palate. He swilled it with his tongue. To success, he thought, and swallowed.

XLII

The second farm the pirates encountered was deserted much like the first. The hearth was warm, and plates were set at the heavy wooden table, but supper was yet to be cooked. Candles were burnt to stubs. "This looks bad," Brio said. "Do you think the island was attacked?"

"Maybe by the Avenger's crew looking for us. We'll have to tread cautiously until we reach the harbor."

"A suggestion, Diego."

"What is that?"

"Half of us continue to the harbor and the other half return to the ship to put the crew on alert."

"Yes, that seems wise." He turned to the men. "Vargas, you, Vasco, and Thomas go back to the Belladonna and put them on alert. Brio, Donald, and I will go on to the town. Wait for me there and do nothing unless you are attacked." Diego stopped suddenly and raised his hand. "Listen." Far below them, there were shouts and gunfire.

Three went back up the slope, and three resumed their descent of the mountainside more wary than ever of what they might find at the bottom.

XLIII

Near midnight, in the narthex, men stood guard, some with muskets, some with axes and sledges. As the night wore on, their nervous tension slipped into weary carelessness. "There's nothing out there," Adrián said, peering into the darkness beyond the torchlit courtyard. The jungle was silent, as if sensing the tension and holding its breath

Antonio leaned against the doorframe. "Father Beppo said there is. Would he lie?"

"No, but nothing is moving. If the moon were brighter, I would feel better. At least I could see someone coming."

"And then what?"

"At least I would know."

Adrián peered once again into the darkness. He heard a sharp cry beside him, and when he turned, Antonio was gone. Then he heard his screams from across the yard. He raised his musket, but could see no target. "Antonio! Antonio!" he cried, but his only answer was more screaming. Other men ran to his side. "What is it?"

The screaming stopped.

"Something has taken Antonio," Adrián said, swinging the musket from side to side and looking over the gun sight.

A loop of rope shot out of the darkness and landed over one of the men. Before he could throw it off himself, the noose tightened around his waist and he was jerked into the darkness, landing on the path outside the church and dragged screaming into the undergrowth. Another *riata* landed over Adrián, but this time his companions wrapped their arms around him and fought the dreadful strength in a deadly tug-of-war, one they were losing inch by inch. A machete flashed in the torchlight, and the rope was cut, sending the islanders tumbling backward into the church.

Father Beppo came running with the rest of the leaders behind. He pulled the doors closed as another lasso bounced off their planking. "You men, hold the door." He looked through the unglazed sidelight and what he saw stunned him. Men, gaunt, ragged, with white eyes were scuttling across the yard. They held axes, pikes, and cutlasses, and behind them, Beppo saw the crimson glow of many pairs of eyes peering through the ferns and brush.

Adrián pushed the muzzle of his musket through the open square at the top of the door. He took aim at one of the attackers and pulled the trigger. Through the puff of smoke, Adrián saw the thing jerk back as the ball hit it full in the chest, yet it kept coming. The shot had no effect.

Overhead, a thumping of feet. The white-eyed devils were on the roof. "The cross!" Beppo shouted. "They're going to take down the cross!"

Cataldo shoved through the crowd of men in the narthex and slammed his shoulder against the doors. They flew open, knocking aside a handful of *trúdovi*. He wrestled free of their clutching hands and ran to the corner of the church, where he seized an overhang and vaulted onto the roof. The palm thatching was tightly laced, but he still had to keep his feet on the beams beneath lest his weight pull him through a weak spot.

On the roof he saw three dim shapes near the peak. One of the attackers was swinging an axe at the base of the cross that jutted from the center of the roof. Cataldo rushed the three, grabbing the first by his shirt and using his momentum to hurl him bodily off the roof. His effort fells short, and the *trúdovi* fell through the thatching and crashed onto one of the benches in the nave.

The fall broke its back, and all it could do was writhe and flail its claws in the air as the people inside shrank back in terror at the sight. It screamed a cross between a panther's snarl and the moan of a soul in Gehenna. One of the men picked up a hammer and struck it in the forehead. He kept pounding the creature until its head was a pulp of brain, bone, and hair.

The second *trúdovi* came at Cataldo with a short pike, narrowly missing his throat with a running thrust. Cataldo grabbed the pike with both hands, hoping to wrest the weapon from the snarling devil, who proved stronger than his bony frame would suggest. The *trúdovi*'s mouth gaped wide, revealing rotting, broken teeth that snapped at Cataldo's fingers as they gripped the pike and breathed the smell of death into his face.

Cataldo twisted hard one way and kicked his opponent's feet aside the other, throwing him down on the fronds. Cataldo's boot heel smashed into the monster's forehead, and he felt the skull give way. The fiend rolled aside and lay still.

The third *trúdovi* hewed at the base of the cross with an axe in one hand while he held on to it with the other. He turned at Cataldo's approach and swung the axe backhanded at him. Cataldo caught the axe hand and

"Something has taken Antonio!"

wrenched the weapon from the *trúdovi's* grip. He raised the blade and brought it down, nearly separating the minion's neck from his shoulders. Blood the color and texture of tar oozed from the wound. The taloned hands dug into Cataldo's shoulders, clawed at his eyes, until Cataldo brought the axe down again, and the *trúdovi's* head rolled down the roof to bounce in the courtyard where the guards were still fruitlessly firing at the attackers.

Cataldo heard a shrill whistle, and below him, he could see the *trúdovi* retreating from the courtyard into the undergrowth. The gunfire ceased, and all was quiet. Suddenly spent, Cataldo sank to his knees on the roof and stared at the cross, spattered with his own red blood and the thick dark blood of the *trúdovi*. He felt his gorge rise and fought it back. His people would not see him shaken.

He shinned down the sloping roof and dropped to the ground in the churchyard. He bent at the waist to lean on one of the gravestones, breathing long draughts of air to clear his head. Someday, one of those slabs would bear his name, but not this day.

XLIV

"What do you think is happening here?" Thomas said, swatting an insistent mosquito on his forearm. "Do you think the Englishmen have landed here looking for us?"

"Perhaps," said Vargas. "But why would the islanders fire on them? It seems insane. The English have more guns and more trained fighters. The islanders are farmers, fishermen, and craftsmen."

"I agree it makes no sense," said Thomas, "but we heard it for ourselves."

Vasco said, "I hope Diego isn't walking into a trap."

"If Pettigrew's men were laying a trap, they wouldn't be firing muskets to alert anyone on the island."

"That's true. In any event, we just have to trust the Hand's good sense and cunning. He's lived this long, and I'm sure he doesn't plan to die this night."

"Sh – listen." Vasco raised his hand.

"What do you hear?" Thomas said.

"It's what I don't hear."

"He's right," said Vargas, pulling his musket from his belt. "The birds and the monkeys are quiet."

It was as if someone had closed a door and shut the jungle noise outside. "Go, but go cautiously. It could be a jaguar."

They moved forward, but more deliberately, Vargas in the lead. They had to be close to the cliff and to the Belladonna now. Just a little longer.

Behind him, Thomas cried out, and at the same time, something broke from the dense ferns to Vargas's right. Instinct took over. Vargas wheeled and fired his pistol. In the powder flare he caught a glimpse of a nightmare. A face, white as a fish belly, its gaping mouth lined with rotting, crooked teeth. Its eyes were as white as its skin, and its hands, curved like claws were reaching for his throat.

Luck was with him. The ball caught the attacker just above his right eye, and in the momentary blindness from the muzzle flash, Vargas heard it fall dead to the ground. Behind him on the path were screams and the sounds of struggle. Vasco's musket went off, fired in the struggle with another of the creatures, its ball ripping through the trees overhead.

In its light, Vargas also saw three of the monsters crouching over Thomas, tearing at his flesh with their talons and their teeth. Thomas no longer screamed.

Vargas drew his cutlass and guessing in the dark, clubbed at what he hoped was the head of Vasco's opponent. He had to strike twice before the stinking thing fell away. "Run," he shouted at Vasco, and Vasco needed no second urging. As they hurried down the path, he said, "Thomas –"

"He's dead," Vargas shot over his shoulder, "and so will we be if we don't get back to the ship."

Behind them, Vargas could hear their pursuers running down the path. They ran so hard that they broke free of the jungle and nearly went over the cliff's edge. In the little light of the crescent moon, Vargas found the handholds carved into the rock and they began their descent.

Above them, Vargas saw the ghastly white faces peering over the cliff's edge. Then one of the white-eyed monsters swung over and began to follow them, crawling backward down the cliff like a spider.

"Damn them," said Vasco, as a second of the devils joined his fellow. "They're climbing down after us."

"Let's hope they can't swim."

The climb was much slower for the pursuers, and Vasco and Vargas reached the rocky shore of the cove long before them. Vargas threw down his sword and pistol and dove into the water. Vasco hesitated but threw down his musket, realizing the folly of trying to swim with it.

Across the cove, they saw the dark shadow of the Belladonna lying at anchor. As they neared the ship, Vargas feared that one of the crew might take a shot at them. "Ho, Belladonna. It's Vargas and Vasco. Don't shoot."

A voice called from the deck, "The parrot speaks."

"But seldom the truth," Vargas replied with the password. "Throw us a rope, quickly."

As they climbed aboard, Vargas heard splashing off the bow.

"Are you being pursued?"

"Yes. By demons." He took a musket from the watchman's hands and cocked the hammer. "Give me a light." One of the pirates shined a lantern over the rail and recoiled at the sight of a gaunt creature in rags climbing the anchor chain. Vargas fired as the creature swung to the right, and the ball hit it in the chest. It jerked backward but kept its grip and in a second, continued to climb.

Another of the creatures clambered over the side and dropped, rolling, to the deck. It rose to a crouch and came scuttling, crab-like across the deck, seizing a crewman in its claws. Vasco grabbed a belaying pin and began to beat the fiend over the head with it. He felt the skull give way, and the creature slumped sideways to the deck.

"There were three of them," Vargas said, looking about.

"There," one of the men said, pointing. In the light of the lantern, they saw the last of the attackers hanging from a rope at the bow. It snarled, and began climbing hand over hand. As its head cleared the railing, Vargas brought an axe down to split its skull. It let go of the rope, and splashed into the water of the cove.

"What in the names of the Saints are those things?"

"I don't know."

"We need to find Diego, warn him," one of the pirates said.

"He said to come here and wait," Vargas answered, "and that's what we will do."

XLV

At sunrise, everyone left the church with a sense of purpose. Men, women, and children all had their jobs to do. The men who had been pulled from the church lay covered with blankets beside Father Beppo's garden. The dead *trúdovi* lay beside them.

"What are they?" Christophe said, staring at the white-eyed creatures. "The hand I found, it is the same as theirs."

"They were once men," said the priest, "But I don't know what has been done to them."

"That is not blood," said Damien, pointing to the dark ichor at the stump of the decapitated *trúdovi 's* neck.

"It is perhaps dead blood," Beppo said.

"But these things do bleed," Cataldo growled. "And they do die. And they are not vampires."

"No," Beppo said, "they are not." He pulled the blanket away and turned Antonio's head by the chin, exposing the puncture marks of fangs at this throat. "But the creatures that killed these men definitely are." He shuddered at the thought of the red eyes he saw glowing in the darkness, kept at bay by the cross and the church. He shuddered again at the thought of what might have happened if the cross had fallen.

"You understand better now the peril we face," Beppo said, staring into the eyes of each of the men in turn. "If it were only vampires, we would be in no peril in the daylight, but these – monsters can move about day or night. So we must be on our guard at all times. We have seen what they did to Esperanza."

"So what must we do?"

"We must gird ourselves for defense."

Cataldo snorted. "No one has attacked the Exiles for a generation, since Montoya and his pirates. Our people don't even remember how to fight."

Beppo shook his head. "But fight we must, if we are going to survive, and if we are not going to perpetuate this evil.

"When the sun set at Armonia, the bodies of the men killed by the fiends rose up. Those bitten die and rise again in a hideous parody of the Resurrection to kill and infect others and make more of their kind. We owe it to ourselves to stay alive, and we owe it to mankind to not become as they are. Those killed by the vampires must be burned."

"There is no other way?" Adrián said.

The *padre* shook his head. "Not that I know to be sure."

"I will see to it."

The men walked away in twos and threes, leaving Father Beppo alone to ponder the most troubling image from the night before. Across the courtyard, in the midst of the attack he had seen a tall aristocratic figure in a long dark coat, his pallid face aglow in the torchlight, standing still amid the chaos, staring into the priest's eyes through the clouds of musket smoke, and smiling.

XLVI

Father Beppo had some of the men bring casks of water to the churchyard. Others brought bags of sea salt culled from evaporating brine. Beppo knew from tradition and lore he had read that holy water was supposed to be effective against vampires. Whether it would work against the undead things that attacked the church the night before was an unknown factor, but common wisdom held that at least the vampires were repelled by it.

He placed a hand on a sack of the salt and held his crucifix before his face. The men around him removed their hats and knelt. "Almighty God, we ask you to bless this salt, as once you blessed the salt scattered over the water by the prophet Elisha. Wherever this salt is sprinkled, drive away the power of evil, and protect us always by the presence of your Holy Spirit. Grant this through Christ our Lord. Amen."

Beppo held out his hand to Christophe. "Your knife." Christophe drew it from its sheath and handed it to the priest, who used it to slit the top of the bag. He thrust his hands in and scooped a double handful. He held it over an open cask of water and carefully sprinkled the salt in the shape of the cross on the surface and repeated the prayer, this time consecrating the water. When he was through, Father Beppo had four casks of holy water and three bags of consecrated salt.

"Padre, why so much salt?" Damien asked.

"Tradition tells us that consecrated salt poured around a house is a protection against evil. I have never known anyone who tested this idea, but now is perhaps the time to find out."

Across the island, Cataldo had a plan of his own taking shape. While men stood guard with muskets, others felled trees to make an abatis. The trees would be embedded in the ground at an angle with their branches sharpened, tangled together, and facing toward the enemy. The palms were useless, but the pines were substantial, plus their branches could be soaked in oil to be lighted if necessary.

We may be taken, Cataldo thought, but they will suffer.

"Cataldo," one of the sentries called out. "Strangers." The guards were all aiming their weapons in the same direction.

Cataldo turned to see three men approaching from the beach, one of them carrying a white rag on the end of a cutlass. As they came closer, Cataldo recognized their leader: Diego lo Mano, The Hand.

The guards stepped out of the tall ferns, muskets aimed at the three pirates. Diego stopped short. "Lower your weapons," he said. "We come in peace."

"No," Cataldo ordered. "Be ready to fire."

Diego had put into Cuerpo Santo twice in the previous three years to take on provisions and he had dealt fairly with Cataldo and his people. His men knew to behave themselves, and he had left on good terms, but in light of the attack the night before, he understood the reception.

"So, you come to palaver?' Cataldo said, confronting Diego. "To work out terms of our surrender?

"Not at all." He thought it better to let Cataldo tell him of the gunfire. "We arrived here last night to trade and provision the Belladonna and we –."

"Lies!" Cataldo pointed his forefinger at Diego. "You led those monsters here to attack our islands so that you can take all that we have."

"Monsters? What monsters? We're running from the British and we came here as we have other times. We have never harmed your people nor stolen from them."

"Liar!" Cataldo came at Diego, hands reaching to clutch his throat.

With a deft flick of his wrist, Diego lowered his flag draped cutlass and Cataldo stopped an inch short of its tip piercing the notch above his breastbone. Hammers cocked. "Shoot me and your *jefe* dies with me." His eyes swept the guards. Everyone held his breath. Diego chose to gamble. "Very well." He drew his pistol from his belt and handed it butt first to Cataldo then stepped back a pace and lowered his sword to the ground. "Now I am unarmed. I pose no threat. Tell me, please what the devil is going on here?"

Cataldo eyed the pirate up and down. "Come with me to Father Beppo." He jerked his head toward Brio and Donald. "You two stay here." Then to his men. "Keep your guns on them. until I return. The rest of you, keep working. I can manage this one."

In the big man's grip, Diego's widow maker looked like a toy. "Walk ahead of me, lo Mano. No tricks."

A dozen paces into the jungle, Diego said over his shoulder, "You know me well enough, Cataldo. We've done business before. I bear you no ill will."

"And you are still a pirate, with allegiance to no flag or people, and for all I know, you would sell your own mother for gold, let alone a group of helpless peasants."

"I heard gunfire as I came down the mountain. Were you attacked by the British ship?"

Cataldo stopped. "What British ship?"

Diego turned to face him. "The Avenger; it's been chasing us for days. We escaped, but I am sure Pettigrew is still looking. I moored the Belladonna on the other side of the island where she can't be seen in the hope that we could conduct our business and move on without jeopardizing ourselves or your people. Did they come ashore?"

"We saw no British ship, but I saw another, a two master named the Votrelec." Cataldo watched Diego's eyes for any sign of guile or of fear.

Diego frowned and shook his head. "Votrelec? I've never heard the name. They attacked you? Pirates?"

"Not pirates – things."

Diego turned his palms upward. "I don't understand."

"Father Beppo will explain." Cataldo cast wary eyes around him. "Keep moving. The church isn't far."

XLVII

Batteaux sat beneath a tree on Armonia's beach. Beyond the shallow cove that comprised Armonia's harbor, the Votrelec lay at anchor. Sebastian's island was indeed deserted. The vampires were on board asleep in their coffins, safe from the rays of the sun. Many of the *trúdovi* were ashore securing the island. Varlek had taken those remaining to Cuerpo Santo where they attacked the islanders seeking refuge in the church. He has his ways and he has his reasons, Batteaux mused. And I can do no more than hear his will and obey. I need not understand.

The *trúdovi* were going through the houses and barns, bringing out whatever was to be found as they searched for people. They were preparing secure resting places for the Anointed as Varlek called his vampire children. To the mindless thralls, a chair was a table was a harp was a chest of gold. They had no sense of value, only of presence, and they heaped all that they found in the village square, a growing mound of trash and treasure.

Batteaux had no idea how Sebastian had raised an alarm, or whether he had at all. Perhaps the dead on Esperanza had been discovered. That would explain the flight from Armonia. He had no doubt the other islands were likewise empty of people.

Whatever had happened, Batteaux was certain that Varlek would deal with it like an axe with a tree. Once the Master set his course, he hesitated at nothing to see it fulfilled. In the meantime, all that Batteaux could do, was labor on in his service in the hope that Varlek would keep his word and free Francine.

Batteaux closed his eyes and let the soft island breezes lull him into a fitful sleep.

He was shaken awake by one of the crew. "Batteaux! Batteaux! Wake up. The Votrelec is sailing away!"

Batteaux scrambled to his feet and looked across the cove to see the Votrelec gliding eastward. Why was Sergi moving? Then he looked to the west and saw the Avenger's sails in the distance. "Get everyone away from the beach and into the trees." The sailor who woke him stared at him, uncomprehending. "Now!"

A standing order among the Votrelec's crew: at the sign of any warship, run. Varlek and his coffin, and those of the Anointed, were to be protected at any cost. That included abandoning any not on board at the moment. Batteaux agreed. To protect Varlek's coffin was to protect Francine.

He anxiously watched the chase ship until it became apparent that it was sailing past Armonia in pursuit of the Votrelec. Perhaps it is just as well, Batteaux thought, for if that ship, whatever flag she flew, landed here, we would have little chance to fend them off.

Batteaux watched until the Votrelec's sails were gone, and the Avenger's sails shrank to a thumbnail on the horizon. He called his men to him. "They may be back. This is what we must do...."

Under Batteaux's direction the crew and the *trúdovi* carried the spoil from the houses to the far side of the island where he had discovered a cave. Spoil was spoil and not to be wasted. It could be barter and bribe should the need arise. If the attack ship were to return, the island would have the appearance of being sacked and deserted.

When the Votrelec returned, and it would, Varlek would decide what should then be done. With their full complement, they could withstand a landing by the crew of a single ship. Now, all he could do was post a watch, and wait.

XLVIII

Brackenridge stared in disbelief at the carnage on Esperanza. Bodies rotting in the blazing sun, beset by the busy gulls and the rats. Their chatter and squawk could be heard all over the island. His men had all seen mass death before, but nothing so hideous as this.

"We have counted twenty-four thus far, sir," said Clark. "No survivors that we can see. The birds have made a bloody mess of them all, but most look as if they've been ripped to pieces."

"lo Mano," said Brackenridge. "He did this. If he needed stores, he could have bought them or stolen them. There was no reason for him to murder everyone."

"Aye, sir. But we'll catch him, and when we do –"

"Yes, Mister Clark, when we do."

The grotesque panorama of Esperanza's village gave Brackenridge a whole new appreciation of Pettigrew's obsession.

"Have the men gather the bodies in front of the chapel and find shovels. These souls will rest in a mass grave, but they will have a proper Christian burial."

"Aye, sir. One other item."

"Yes, Mister Clark?"

"None of the houses or barns was damaged, but the chapel has been smashed proper inside. Why would they do that?"

"I am beyond pondering such questions. See to the burial."

By noon, the crewmen had dug a pit in the center of the village. Brackenridge insisted that each be laid in gently, arms folded across their chests, not carelessly tossed into the hole like offal. These were, after all, human beings, and as such, they deserved their dignity, even in death.

When the last of the dead was in the grave, Brackenridge gave the nod, and the men began shoveling dirt over the bodies, to the outraged squawking of the gulls. One of the men had fashioned a cross from a pair of wooden slats, and in absence of names cut twenty-six notches, the final total, into the upright and drove it into the ground with the blade of his shovel.

Brackenridge spoke the prayer, modified from the seaman's burial. That done, thought Brackenridge, it is time to seek justice.

XLIX

On the Votrelec, a cry came from the crow's nest. "Sail!"

Sergi shielded his eyes with a hand and saw the ship. He raised the telescope, and his eye found the Avenger coming full speed.

"All hands," he bellowed. "Make sail." The crew understood and in minutes, the Votrelec's anchor was raised, and she was racing east at an oblique angle away from Armonia. Sergi looked back to the Avenger and saw that the ship was changing course. His first priority was to escape if he could; failing that, his second, fight if he must; failing that, his third, protect the Master to the end of his life.

L

"Sail!"

The cry from overhead brought Brackenridge to the foredeck. The Avenger was heading for Armonia, the next island in line. "Is it the Belladonna, Mister Berks?"

"Too far to tell as yet, sir."

"Then let us find out. Inform the helmsman."

"Aye, sir."

If the ship allows itself to be overtaken, Brackenridge thought, then we move on, but if she runs, then we chase her with all that we've got and hope the Hand is at the helm.

"Mister, Cadwell."

"Aye, sir."

"Ready the long nine."

"Aye sir."

At Cadwell's order, the gun crew scurried to load and prepare the long nine, a chase gun with a long barrel in the Avenger's bow that fired a lighter ball than the guns at the ports. "As soon as we're in range, lo Mano," Brackenridge muttered, "we'll put a niner right up your bloody arse."

LI

When Diego rounded the bend into the village, he saw it was as busy as an anthill. People scurried in every direction carrying anything and everything imaginable. Most of the people he saw in the village square were women and children. In a moment he understood why. The men were busily turning the church into a fortress. Barricades were erected, pointed stakes driven into the ground to resist attackers, and men with shovels and mattocks digging a shallow, narrow moat around the church.

"You look as if you expect an invasion," Diego said as they stepped through a break in the barricade that was rising around the building.

Ignoring him, Cataldo stopped a man who was carrying a heavy beam across his shoulders. "Where is Father Beppo?"

The man eyed Diego as he would any stranger then saw the pistol in Cataldo's hand. "In the churchyard, last time I saw him."

Cataldo gestured with the widow maker. "That way."

Diego saw the priest standing before open casks filled with water. He was sprinkling what looked like sand or salt into one of them. As Diego came closer, he saw the priest was laying out the shape of a cross on the surface.

Diego turned to Cataldo. "What –?"

Cataldo held up a hand for silence. The priest intoned a prayer and crossed himself. Diego could see by his posture and the look on his face that the old man was weary, but his eyes were alive. He took Diego's measure at once. "Who is this man, Cataldo?"

"Diego lo Mano, Father; the Hand, the pirate and reaver. He says his ship came here last night but he claims to know nothing about the attack."

"And a customer who has traded honestly with this island in the past."

Beppo's eyebrows raised, and he shot a look at Cataldo. "This is so? You do business with this man, although he is a pirate?"

Diego smiled. "The Savior at his crucifixion promised the thief beside him that he would see him in Paradise. If the Lord does not discriminate…" He shrugged.

Cataldo looked away. "His gold is as good as anyone's."

Beppo walked all around Diego, studying him. When the priest was again before him, he raised his cross inches from Diego's face. Diego did not flinch. "Say the Lord's Prayer."

Diego hesitated and heard Cataldo cock the pistol. "*Padre nuestro, que etas en el cielo, sanctificado sea tu nombre... .*" Diego finished the prayer, and Beppo said, "Now, cross yourself."

Diego did with neither difficulty nor unusual consequence. Beppo turned to Cataldo and nodded.

"That means nothing, *Padre*," Cataldo said. "This man is a pirate, he could be simply working with them as a human, doing their bidding, things they could not do."

"As a human?" Diego said. "What else could I be?"

Beppo stared into Diego's eyes. "The undead."

"Undead?"

"Vampires."

Diego turned his palms up. "I know nothing of any vampires. Are you saying that is what attacked your island?"

"That and more," Cataldo said. "And you may have a hand in it."

"That's my widow maker you're holding. Would I have given it to you if that were so? Either believe me or shoot me, Cataldo."

"I believe you," Beppo said. The priest gave a quick account of all that had passed the previous two days up to the moment, the dead on Armonia and Esperanza, the missing children, the attack, and the mysterious ship.

Votrelec," Diego mused. "Not a name I know. You think that these things that attacked you came from that ship?"

"Where else?" Cataldo said. "They could have come from nowhere but the sea."

The priest concluded by uncovering the bodies of the dead *trúdovi*.

"Your people killed these creatures?"

"I killed two of them," Cataldo said, a finger pointing to his chest.

"Last night, as my men and I came down the mountain, we heard gunfire. This was the attack?"

"The guns were ours," the priest said. "Not theirs."

"The guns did nothing," Cataldo said. "Men shot these creatures, but to no effect. I killed these two; one I beheaded with his own axe. The other, I crushed his skull."

Beppo continued, "Your ship is moored here?"

Diego nodded. "In the cove at the eastern tip of the island."

"Then your crew is in peril. You must go to them and bring them here for safety."

"Padre, if anyone – or anything attacks the Belladonna, he will have his hands full."

"Perhaps," Beppo said. "Perhaps."

"If lo Mano's not in league with them, maybe he'll just sail away and wash his hands of us and save his own neck."

Ignoring Cataldo, Father Beppo put his hands on Diego's shoulders. "By now, I am sure the evil knows you are here, Diego. If you run, when it is finished with us, it will pursue you to safeguard its unholy secret, and I have no doubt it will find you. And if you run, our blood will be on your hands, and you will carry that burden with you to Purgatory. We do not battle for our lives only. The Savior said, 'Fear not those who kill the body but cannot destroy the soul.' These creatures can do both."

"I will return to my ship and let my crew make their decision. They will follow me against any man, but I cannot order them to fight demons."

"I understand. If you are going, do so quickly. These creatures can attack in daylight or darkness and if they know of your ship, your crew is in danger."

Diego turned to Cataldo. "To climb back over the mountain will take hours. Lend me a boat that my men and I can sail around the island quickly."

Cataldo balked, but Beppo said simply. "Do it."

"All right. Come with me."

"Godspeed, my son. I know you will make the right decision."

As they returned to Diego's men on the beach, Cataldo said, "Some show you put on there. When was the last time you set foot in a church?"

"When was the last time you took confession?"

Cataldo glared at him and walked on.

On the beach, Diego found Donald and Brio sitting back to back on the sand under the watchful eyes and muzzles of two of the guards. "Release them and return their weapons," Cataldo said. He called one of the guards over. "Take these men to the harbor and give them a small boat to sail around the island on my authority."

The guard nodded and asked no questions. So much had happened since the previous sunrise, he no longer questioned anything.

"I will be pleased if I see you again, lo Mano, and surprised."

"The only reason you'll be pleased is that if you see me, you'll still be alive."

Cataldo gave a bitter laugh. "If the *Padre* is right and we are dealing with vampires, perhaps I will be dead, and I will be pleased to see you anyway."

Diego felt a chill course through him like a snake in his entrails. "We will see what we will see."

Cataldo handed Diego's pistol back to him. "You'll need this."

That said, Diego and his friends followed the guard down the beach toward the harbor.

"He's a hard one, that Cataldo," Brio said.

Diego nodded. "Aye, but suited well for the task at hand."

LII

Within two hours, the Avenger began to close on the Votrelec. Through his telescope, Sergi could finally recognize the British colors flapping from the mast. British, likely thinking the Votrelec was a Corsair ship, he thought.

One of the crew came beside him. "She's a faster vessel, Sergi. We can't outrun her, and she's got us outmanned and outgunned. We couldn't survive a boarding."

"I have an idea."

LIII

Brackenridge and Berks stood in the bow of the Avenger. Soon, he would be within firing range of the fleeing ship. The name across the stern was nearly obliterated by time; Brackenridge could barely make out the name Votrelec. She flew no flag nor pennon, and he could see now that it was not the Belladonna, but duty bound him to give chase. Cadwell's men stood at the ready to fire the long nine.

Movement on deck. Brackenridge scanned the stern of the enemy vessel with his telescope and saw children, a dozen or more, being lined up across the railing, held by gaunt men in ragged clothing. A hulking brute with a thick beard stood behind them.

Without warning, the bearded man picked up one of the children and heaved him over the side to splash in the ship's wake.

In a moment, another child was thrown into the sea, this time a small girl.

"You'll need this."

"Damn and blast!" Brackenridge shouted. "The monsters!"

"What do we do, sir?"

A third child went over the railing. Brackenridge thought of his own children at home in Liverpool. All right, he thought, it's not the Belladonna. "Reef," he said. "Prepare to pick up survivors."

"Aye, sir."

"Whoever captains that ship is a shrewd devil, Mister Berks."

"Aye sir, and a vicious one."

LIV

The Votrelec finally pulled away from the Avenger. Varlck would not be pleased to lose even a handful of the captive children, but there were always more to be had; small price for his safety. Once the Avenger's sails were no longer in sight, Sergi set a course to circle back to Armonia. When Varlek woke, Sergi would explain what had happened. Of course, he thought, Varlek will probably know without being told.

The ship would have to pick up Batteaux's group of *trúdovi* on the island and then would have to immediately put distance between themselves and Armonia, in case the gunship returned. The Votrelec may have held its own against the newcomer in ordinary circumstances, but in daylight and with half the crew ashore, it seemed a bad risk. Protecting the Master was paramount, and that is what he did.

LV

The sailboat made its way to the east side of the island without incident, and Diego rounded the spit of land to the cove where the lookout recognized him and signaled the crew of the Belladonna to hold their fire. In minutes he was climbing aboard his ship.

"When you didn't come back, we thought you were dead," Pike told him.

"We nearly were. There is trouble in the Exiles."

"The Avenger?"

"No, something else. Something worse." He quickly told his officers about the island's peril and the priest's call for help. When he finished,

Vargas told him of what they had encountered.

"Call everyone on deck."

In minutes, The Belladonna's crew stood before Diego. He asked for rum, and a flask was passed to him. He took a deep pull on it, wiped his mouth with the back of his hand, and spoke.

"We have traveled around this world more than once together. We have fought many battles, celebrated many victories. We have seen many strange things. Today, I have seen one of the strangest I have ever encountered.

"The Exiles are under attack, not by our nemesis, the Avenger, but by something the likes of which I have never seen. The undead."

Murmurs broke out among the crew. "Shut your mouths, all of you," Pike shouted. "Listen to the Captain."

The noise died down and Diego continued. "I've heard the stories; we all have, about men brought back from the dead. Today I learned that those stories are true.

"An evil army has attacked the islands. I have seen two of their dead, and if they were once men, they are men no longer."

"As have I," said Vargas.

"And I," Vasco added.

Diego continued. "The fiends have taken the children and murdered everyone else on Esperanza. They have abducted women, and they have attacked the islanders who are taking refuge in Cuerpo Santo's church.

"Father Beppo, and Cataldo, Cuerpo Santo's *jefe* have asked for our help in defending the island and the people. I know you would follow me into battle against any man, flag, or navy, but I cannot expect you to follow me against an army of darkness." Diego paused. "Besides the undead, there are vampires."

Murmuring broke out again, and Diego had to shout to be heard, "We are far from saints. We have robbed, pillaged, and killed, but we have never defiled a church. And we have never slaughtered innocent people. These islanders have been our friends. We have traded with them in good faith, and they have protected us in the past. Perhaps we have been given the chance to redeem our souls. The question is, do we fight to help these people, or do we run?"

There was a long silence. Diego's gaze swept his crew. "I am for fighting. Who is with me?"

"How do we kill things that are already dead?" one of the men asked.

"Cataldo killed two of them last night in the fighting. Vasco and Vargas killed three on this ship. They can be stopped."

"But vampires?"

"We have never seen them before, but we've all heard the legends. They are powerful, but not invincible."

Brio stepped beside Diego. "If the Hand says fight, I say we fight."

Pike added his voice. "I'm for it."

"Any man among you who wants to take his share and leave, do so now with my blessing. I won't condemn you, because we may all die, and some of us may be turned into those creatures, but if you stay with me, we fight to the end. Who is with me?"

Fists raised, a few at first, but in waves of greater numbers until the whole joined in. "We'll fight the Devil himself beside you, Captain," one of the crew shouted.

"And by God, we'll beat him," shouted another.

A cheer rose from the crew, and Diego raised his hands. "A man could ask for no better than the lot of you. Let us fight to win."

LVI

As the shadows grew long, the Votrelec returned to Armonia, but not to its harbor. The ship lay at anchor on the opposite side of the island, hoping to avoid the eyes of the gunship that pursued her earlier. Sergi sent a small crew ashore in a longboat to alert Batteaux.

There was still work to be done to establish an operating base. Sergi was a man of the sea, but willing to follow the Master's lead in exchange for the promised wealth and power an island kingdom would provide for all of them. The alternative was to be turned into one of the white-eyed *trúdovi*, and serve mindlessly until blood rot ate away muscle and sinew, leaving only corroded, misshapen bones.

For three years, Sergi had piloted the Votrelec, taken her through storms that would have smashed most ships to splinters, fought running battles with buccaneers, and evaded capture by privateers and naval vessels who thought the Votrelec itself to be a pirate ship.

His success was not rewarded in gold, for where would he spend it? Instead, Varlek offered rewards that could not be measured in coin. The first time he sailed the Votrelec through a hurricane that threatened to turn the ship upside down, the vampire lord honored him with a gift beyond imagining.

Varlek came to his cabin late that night. "You have served me well, Sergi," the vampire said, "and I am one whose generosity equals his gratitude." From behind him slipped a golden haired woman clad in gossamer veils that drifted about her sinuous body like fingers of lavender smoke. Her eyes glowed in the brassy lamplight, and her irises seemed to change color like the passing of clouds.

Sergi stood mesmerized at the sight as she spun and strutted around his cabin, giving him a tantalizing glimpse of breast, thigh, and buttock when he could pull his gaze from her penetrating eyes. She wound herself around him, teasing his lips with hers, until he took her in a rough embrace and pressed his mouth to her.

Her tongue slithered between his lips, hot and firm, and seemed to slide over his and down his throat until it reached his loins and made his manhood as firm as the ship's main mast. Still he stared into the temptress' eyes and watched the colors swirl and blend. He never heard the door to his cabin close as Varlek left.

Sergi spent his night in the throes of an ecstasy that threatened to cross the boundaries into sheer agony as she ground at him endlessly, and he never relaxed nor relented, his mind lost to him as she looted the depths of his soul. She held him through the night in a constant euphoria teetering on the aching knife edge between anticipation and satisfaction. Then, as the dawn approached, she allowed him release, and he fell back onto his bunk, spent physically and emotionally.

The succubus drifted away, and as he slipped into unconsciousness, Sergi heard Varlek's voice echo in the empty chambers of his mind, "All this and more for those who serve me."

And for that pleasure, Sergi would serve the Devil himself, if he were not already.

LVII

In his cabin, Sebastian stared at the walls around him. Varlek had used him and put him away, and would no doubt use him again. He had felt a rush of exhilaration when Armonia was found deserted, but knew that the terror was far from over. There were only so many places the islanders could have gone, and Varlek would likely not stop until he found them.

Something had happened. The ship had been anchored at Armonia, and had suddenly set sail and done so at high speed, the bow slapping hard on the waves below his cabin. He thought of Jada and his son Dominic, and his grandchildren, despairing of ever seeing them alive again. Sebastian closed his eyes and said a prayer, begging that if he never saw his family alive again, for the Lord to spare him the sight of them returned to life as white-eyed, rotting devils.

LVIII

The logistics of rescue were nerve wracking. The Avenger approached the first of the children, floundering panic-stricken in the water and lowered a boat, then moved on to the next several hundred yards away. Brackenridge had watched the bastard heave five children over the stern and he felt compelled to save them all.

Five children to rescue. The first four were a success as Brackenridge watched the sails disappear in the distance, but by the time they reached the place where the fifth had been thrown, instead of a splashing child, he saw the circling of fins and realized he was too late.

On board, the children were in a state of shock. They stared wide-eyed at something far beyond the horizon and did not speak.

They huddled in a semicircle on the deck wrapped in blankets. Brackenridge squatted before them. "Who did this to you?" he asked. The oldest, a dark haired Spanish boy of perhaps ten years, opened his mouth. It gaped open and shut like a fish on a dock, and finally a word came out. "*Monstruos.*"

"Take the children below, Mister Clark. See that they're fed and cared for in every way."

"Aye sir."

Brackenridge stared across the water. He now had two sharks to reel in. And he would succeed if it took him the rest of his life. He had seen evil in many forms, but never flaunted so brashly.

Monsters indeed.

LIX

Diego decided that the quickest course was the safest. He chose to sail around Cuerpo Santo and deploy most of his men at the harbor, then with a skeleton crew, bring the Belladonna back to the cove for concealment.

He stood by the helm. The crew was resolute; their initial enthusiasm had ebbed as the reality of the task set in. They were committed, but Diego could sense the tension as they prepared to set sail. They were grimly determined and would not flee the fight, and Diego felt the same pang as any general, captain, or warlord leading men into a battle: how many of the faces he saw on deck would not live to see the next day or to sail away when the battle was through.

He had fought the ships of every navy in Europe, fought privateers and other pirates, and the rag tag militias of coastal provinces, and known what to expect: cannon, muskets, and swords. This battle was something more, something shrouded in shadows and evil. As Father Beppo had said, they would be fighting not only for their lives, but for their souls. He would have prayed, but Diego had been a thief and a killer for so long, that he doubted his prayers would be heard. Let the priest pray for them all.

LX

"What do you think?" Clark, the surgeon said. He sat with Brackenridge at the table in his cabin. "Why the children?"

"Sell them into slavery, mayhap," said Brackenridge.

Clark nodded. "It's been done before."

"Aye," said Brackenridge. "But if they were the ship's treasure, why would he sacrifice them so easily?"

"Maybe to just save his skin and his ship. There are always more children."

"Or perhaps the ship had something of greater value to protect." Brackenridge tamped the tobacco in his pipe. "I wonder what that could be."

"We'll know when we catch him," Clark said.

"If we do," said Brackenridge resignedly. "The Carribees are a grand haystack to search for a needle."

A knock at the cabin door. Beckwith, Clark's assistant brought the children in and seated them at the table. All had been fed, and washed and given what clothing could cover them. The children were more than docile; they seemed totally devoid of any emotion or self-direction. All stared ahead at nothing.

Brackenridge asked them again what happened to them and who were the men who had taken them prisoner. No response. He set a bowl of bananas and mangoes before them. None moved or even seemed to notice the fruit.

For a time, none of the children spoke. Brackenridge sat silent as well, letting the void do its work. Finally one of them hesitantly opened her mouth, a girl no older than seven or eight years. She was a short, stocky child whose face bore the same dull expression of shock and trauma as the others.

"White-eyes," she whispered, almost inaudible. "The white-eyes came from the sea and they took us away."

Clark opened his mouth to say something, but Brackenridge put a restraining hand on his arm.

"They took us to a big boat and put us below in a room with bars."

"The brig," said Clark. Brackenridge nodded.

"No food, no water."

"Yes, child," Clark said, "and what happened then?"

"At night the red-eyes came." The girl's eyes widened. "They reached through the bars for us, they caught Sonya." Her voice rose to a shriek, "And they bit her! They bit her!" She rocked back and forth in the chair, screaming.

Clark tried to hold the girl, but she leapt from the chair and began flailing. The other children, spurred by her outburst began screaming as well.

"Take them to a cabin with windows," Brackenridge said. "Make them as comfortable as you can."

"Should I give them laudanum?" Clark asked. "It may give them some peace."

"Perhaps so," Brackenridge said over the wails of the children.

Clark and Beckwith took the children away with the help of other crewmen, leaving Brackenridge to ponder the girl's story. White-eyes, red-eyes, monsters. The story made no sense, but to the eye of childhood, any adult who causes harm is a monster larger than life.

Brackenridge sat back in his chair and stared out the windows of his cabin at the sea. He was beginning to reconsider his priorities. He wanted to bring the Hand to justice, but perhaps he should be chasing the Votrelec instead. No, he thought, one devil at a time. I'll find lo Mano and then I'll chase down that bearded animal and show him what happens to cowards who harm innocent children.

LXI

In the late afternoon, Diego brought the Belladonna around the island to the port and anchored far enough offshore to be able to run at the first sign of the Avenger. He sent most of his crew ashore, leaving enough men to return the ship to the cove. With the men, he brought ashore muskets, powder, and shot, and one thing more. When he rode the last longboat to the harbor, an iron bound chest lay at his feet. The pirates had culled the silver from the gold and other spoil and sunk those chests to the bottom of the cove.

Beppo had told him that silver was one weapon against the vampires. If thirty pieces of silver bought death for the savior, surely three hundred would be proof against the vampire horde.

Diego watched as the Belladonna sailed away, with Brio at the helm. He hated to leave his ship in the hands of another, but he realized that if his men were going to fight, he should be beside them, shoulder to shoulder. Brio would care for the ship as if it were his own child. The priest was right. A man cannot unsee what he has seen, nor forget so monstrous an evil. Now that he knew of it, it would follow him to the ends of the earth to destroy him.

The greatest trick of the Devil, Diego thought, is to make people believe that he doesn't exist, and so too with the vampire. So long as people thought he was legend, myth, fairy tale, they would be unwary and vulnerable.

"Why would the vampires attack the Exiles?" Pike said, breaking into Diego's thoughts.

"Opportunity, perhaps. They are isolated, and their protection from Spain is as haphazard as their blessings from the Church. The name, the Exiles, fits their situation as well as it does their islands. They fled persecution and became their own world. And now, after generations have passed, they are like castaways who have become resigned to fending for themselves. That ship Cataldo saw – it could be the vampires' conveyance from feeding ground to feeding ground."

"Aye, they could hardly put into Havana and go on shore leave. Yet, perhaps there is more here than opportunity."

"Such as what?"

"That I don't know, Diego, but I suspect we will find out."

At the church, the fortifications were all but complete. The abatis ringed the church, limbs hewn to spear points, twisted and woven among each other to form what looked to be an impenetrable barrier. The sharpened trunks of trees looked like fingers reaching through a tangle of wild brambles, or perhaps the quills of a porcupine; equally sharp and menacing.

"Not exactly a *chevaux-de-freise*, but effective. They did all this in one day?" Pike said, looking around him at the defenses.

"Yes," Diego replied. "Most of this was not here this morning."

"If I had a crew like that, I could do anything."

"Survival is the greatest motivation."

"Aye, that and a lusty woman." At Diego's look, Pike shrugged. "If we can't laugh, we're lost."

As they stepped over the dry narrow moat inside the abatis, Christophe greeted them. "Thank God you've come to help."

"What can we do?"

"The outer barricade is nearly complete. Men are behind the churchyard now, cutting down the trees to keep attackers from dropping to the ground inside the abatis."

"That is a good strategy. I'll have my men help you."

Christophe hurried off, and Pike said, "It appears they've done this before."

"But not for a long time, judging by the size of the trees they're cutting. Twenty years, give or take."

"What?"

"Cataldo said that they held off an attack by Montoya. That was the last time they had to mount a defense against anyone."

"The Black Dagger? He's been dead at least that long."

"If they survived his cutthroats, they're more than just simple fishermen and farmers."

"They're schooled in defense," Pike said, "but defense against men."

"True enough, but you'll see that the priest knows more than most about the enemy."

"I hope so," Pike shuddered. "I truly don't fancy fighting demons, but I know you wouldn't lead us into a fight if there were no chance of beating the devils."

If only that were true, Diego thought. If only that were true.

Father Beppo saw them and crossed the churchyard. "You came back, my son. I knew you would."

"*Padre,*" Diego said, "where is the town's forge?"

Beppo pointed. "Not far. That way beyond the stables."

"Stables? I didn't know you had horses."

"We have no horses, but we have oxen and two burros."

Diego rubbed his chin. "They will be useful. Have some of your men bring them here and tie them to trees at different points outside the barricade."

"Why, Diego?" said Pike.

The old priest smiled. "Have you never heard the tale of the Battle of the Allia?"

Pike shook his head. "I don't know much about history, Father."

"Livy tells us, the invaders, the Senones, discovered a shepherd's path to climb the mount behind the city and planned to swoop down on it and surprise the Romans while they slept. They were stealthy, and the Centurions on watch did not hear the attackers, nor did the dogs. They were heard instead by the geese sacred to the goddess Juno, whose honking woke the Romans. The animals will alert us when anyone or anything approaches."

"And for the forge, *Padre.*" Diego waved to two of his men who carried the iron bound chest between them. They set it on the ground, and Diego opened the lid. In it were coins, jewelry, a pair of goblets, and a candlestick, all silver.

"You said silver is proof against the vampire. My smith will melt this down and recast it as musket balls and shot for our guns and yours. If they come, they will not have an easy victory."

Beppo shouted to Raoul, "Where is Tomás? Bring him to me."

In a moment, Raoul returned with a man whose arms were as thick as Diego's thighs.

"This is Tomás Flora, our metal smith." He turned to the smith. "Take these men to your forge at once."

"Si, Padre."

"But first—" Beppo pulled a flask from his robe and sprinkled its contents on the treasure. "*In nomine de Patri,...*" Beppo blessed the silver then said, "Go quickly. In a few hours the sun will set."

LXII

As the sun sank below the horizon, Sergi guided the Votrelec into Armonia's harbor. Soon Varlek would wake and demand answers. That the Russian had kept him safe should satisfy the Master, although his safety came at a price. Sergi was fortunate that the pursuing ship, The Avenger, he had read on her bow, ceased pursuit at the fifth child. He gambled and won, guessing the proper British sailors would not ignore the plight of children. If they realized that the plight of those still on board was far worse than those in the water, they may not have abandoned the chase.

The last edge of the sun's red coin dropped below the horizon, and without looking, Sergi knew that Varlek was standing at his side. "Sergi." the vampire's voice slithered around the inside of his skull. "Why are we not unloaded?" Before he could reply, Varlek said, "I know the answer, but I want to hear it from your lips."

"A ship. A British ship called the Avenger pursued us. I had only half a crew to sail at speed and to man the guns. I ran to protect you and the Votrelec from capture."

Sergi turned and saw the Master's saturnine face elongate and twist into his true visage. He had seen it many times before, and it no longer frightened him. What did however was the rage that radiated from the vampire's face. "The British. It has been many years since I tasted the blood of an Englishman. Before this night is over, we will find this Avenger and pay her captain a visit. I will show him what happens to people who interfere in my plans, and I will show him the meaning of true vengeance."

LXIII

The shadows deepened, and the islanders crowded once again into the church. Outside, the pirates manned the barricade side by side with the local defenders, many armed with muskets and pistols from the Belladonna. With Tomás' help, Diego's men were able to cast enough silver into musket balls and scatter shot for most of the guns. Those were to be fired at vampires only. For the white-eyes, axes, machetes, and cutlasses were honed to a shaving edge.

Cataldo's instructions were clear. "The white-eyes are strong. They are not easy to kill, but it can be done. They quit fighting when you behead them or crush their skulls. I learned that last night. The best time to deal with them is while they are tangled in the branches of the abatis."

Diego spoke up. "And if they get over the barricade, you men with the blades swing for their knees. Cut off a leg and they won't be able to move so well. If they crawl, cut off an arm."

"Those of you with rosaries and crosses, wear them to be seen." Father Beppo said. "They will hold off the vampires. Remember, the Savior is watching over us, but we must do our part of it. In his words, 'The Lord helps those who help themselves.'"

When the men took their positions, instead of going into the church, Father Beppo remained in the courtyard. "You are not going inside, *Padre*?" Diego asked.

"This is The Lord's house," Beppo said, a fierce look in his eyes from the brassy glow of the torches. He picked up a machete and wrapped a rosary tightly around the handle at the guard. "I will die before I allow any of those creatures to defile it."

"And now," Pike said looking beyond the barricade into the quickly merging shadows, "we wait."

"I'd rather be fighting," said Diego.

"So would I." Pike said. "Waiting makes me wearier than a good battle."

And they stared past the torchlit courtyard into the gathering darkness, straining eyes and ears for any trace of intruders, overhead through the opening in the foliage, the eternal stars looked on, impassive and silent.

"Look," said Renaldi, one of Diego's crew. He pointed upward. "The Southern Cross."

The men gazed skyward at the constellation, which seemed to outshine the other stars.

"It is a sign," the priest said, crossing himself. "It is the brazen serpent in the wilderness. Look upon it and live."

"I hate to sound like a heathen, Father," Pike said, "but if we want to live, we'd best be watching the earth, not the heavens."

LXIX

The Avenger lay at anchor off Paz. Brackenridge decided that it was too risky to land and search the island at night, so they would wait until dawn and take the Marines ashore. The day's events shook him to his core. The horrors of Esperanza were sufficient to fill a man's dreams with fright for the rest of his days, but the sight of the bearded sailor throwing the children from the unnamed ship haunted him more.

Brackenridge slumped in his chair. He recalled a book he had seen as a boy. It was a favorite of his in his father's library. It was an atlas, colorful maps of the continents and oceans of the world. He would pore over them for hours, imagining the lands they outlined. But his greatest fascination lay in the depiction of the uncharted oceans of the New World. Great blank spaces some with the foreboding words, "Here there be monsters."

The maps showed winged dragons breathing fire, scaly horned lizards, and sea serpents like the seven-headed beast of Revelation, but none, thought Brackenridge, could match the evil he had seen that day.

A knock.

"Yes."

It was Clark. "The children are all sleeping, William."

"Better than I'll do this night. Perhaps you should give me laudanum too."

"No less for myself."

Brackenridge refilled his brandy and poured another for Clark then motioned for him to sit. "What do you make of their tale, William?"

"Something the boy said a short while ago; I barely heard it, he spoke so low. It sounded as if he said Esperanza."

Brackenridge sat upright in his chair. "Esperanza? That would explain why we found no bodies of children among the dead. All were taken captive."

"And that would exonerate the Hand, at least for that atrocity."

"Let's not be too quick to pardon lo Mano. Perhaps they were working in league with each other."

"Have you ever known the Hand to partner with anyone else?"

Brackenridge shook his head. "No, but if he were desperate enough, with us about to take him, who knows what measures he might employ."

"It's a difficult fence you straddle, William."

"How many years have we served together?'

"A good dozen."

"Have you ever known me to be indecisive?"

Clark gave a short barking laugh. "What an absurd question."

"At this moment, I am torn between two objectives. lo Mano and this phantom ship full of child killers."

"Which of the two is more likely to be here, at the Exiles?"

"lo Mano. The Belladonna needs to be re-provisioned and that's something pirates can't do in the light of day with a chase ship prowling around. I'm betting he and his men are lying low and waiting for their chance to restock their supplies then escape. The nameless ship is likely far away by now and we may never see her again, although in my heart, I pray that we do."

"Then perhaps you should take the prize nearest to hand."

"Perhaps you're right."

Clark finished his brandy and stood. "We should both try to get some sleep, William. God knows neither of us will be of much use without it."

"Good night, William."

"Good night." Clark left the cabin and closed the door behind him. The night was shrouded in mist. He looked around the deck and saw no one on watch. He had passed Jenkins just a few moments before and spoken to him, now Jenkins was gone. Breedwell was nowhere in sight either. Clark's foot slipped on the deck and he looked down. A puddle of water surrounded a green rope of seaweed. Further down the deck, he saw an arm barely visible behind a hatchway.

It was Jenkins. He was lying face down on the deck, and Clark rolled him over. In the dim light, Clark saw that the right side of his throat was savagely torn out.

He put his hand over his mouth, stepped to the rail to vomit, and looked over to see a horde of pale-skinned red-eyed creatures climbing from the dark water up the lines and the anchor chain. Behind him they clambered over the starboard rail. Clark opened his mouth to sound an alarm, but before he could cry out, taloned hands clamped around his neck. He was jerked backward and felt a wave of pain as fanged jaws closed on his throat, spat out a gobbet of flesh, and left him spurting blood on the planking.

In seconds, the deck of the Avenger was swarming with the undead as more and more climbed aboard. They rushed down the gangways and dropped into the hold. The crewmen woke to a fight they could never have dreamed. Sailors and Marines were torn from their hammocks and

"Have you ever known me to be indecisive?"

summarily savaged by the red-eyed attackers. Fangs and claws ripped their flesh. Cruel hands snapped their necks and left them flopping on the blood slick deck like beached fish.

This was no feeding frenzy; it was pure murder. Shots were fired, knives were drawn, but to no avail. Men were yanked from their hammocks before they could climb to their own defense to be separated from their souls by the fanged monsters.

In his cabin, Brackenridge heard the melee and pulled a brace of pistols from the wall. He opened his cabin door to see a dark shape with glowing eyes before him. The huge, black invader opened its mouth to bare a ripsaw set of fangs. Brackenridge fired one pistol then the other between those eyes, but they had no effect.

The fiend seized him by the arms, lifted him from the floor and dashed across the cabin to slam him into the bulkhead. Once, twice, and on the third strike, Brackenridge slumped unconscious to the floor.

Water in his face woke him a few moments later. He found himself staring into the eyes of the bearded giant who threw the children overboard. "You!" Brackenridge tried to scramble to his feet but was held down by several pairs of hands. He turned his head and recoiled in horror at the sight of a gaunt figure dressed in rags with dead white eyes. His head whipped around, and he saw that more like that one were pinning him to the cabin floor. His head spun. White eyes, red eyes.

The door opened and Varlek strode in, dressed in a ruffled shirt, violet brocade vest, and a long black velvet coat. His pale face showed what looked like amusement at Brackenridge's plight. The vampire studied him for a moment, forefinger to his chin.

"I am Varlek. You are –"

"William Brackenridge, acting Captain of His Majesty's ship the Avenger," he snarled.

Varlek turned to Sergi. "Bring him on deck."

Sergi spoke words in a language Brackenridge had never heard, and the *trúdovi* lifted him roughly to his feet. He struggled, but found the creatures' grip as firm as manacles. They dragged him onto the deck, where he saw bodies of his slain crew piled in a heap. Beyond the rail, he saw the lights of another ship, the Votrelec, riding at anchor to port.

"You have interfered in my plans, *Captain*." A sneer was implicit in Varlek's tone. "That I cannot abide. To ensure that you will not interfere again, I have disposed of most of your crew. Only a handful remain alive."

Varlek gestured, and the flame-eyed vampires brought twelve men on deck from below. They put the crewmen in a line and Varlek said, "I have left you twelve, a meaningful number. So many things come in twelves; months of the year, signs of the Zodiac, twelve pairs of ribs in the human skeleton, twelve tribes of Israel, twelve apostles...

"But before I deal with them, I want to reclaim my property. Sergi."

The bearded brute accompanied by more of the white eyes brought the children on deck.

"These are mine," Varlek said. "They were lost, and you found them, but now I am taking them back." His hand caressed the face of a little girl, who cringed away, wide eyed in terror.

"Leave them alone. They're innocent. They've never done a thing to you."

"You presume to tell me what to do?" Varlek's eyes blazed. "I'm not one of your Jack tars to order about the deck." To Brackenridge's horror, the vampire took the child by her arm and leg and lifted her bodily to his gaping mouth and plunged his fangs into the screaming girl's neck and drank, all the while, holding Brackenridge's eyes with his gaze. When he finished, he dropped the child's body now a lifeless husk, on the deck.

Varlek licked the blood from his lips in obvious relish. "Now, *Captain*, he said, "I will leave you with your ship – and your crew." He gestured to the heap of bodies on the deck. "I spare your life, not because I am merciful, but because I am cruel and can think of no greater punishment. But first, my minions deserve their reward."

He gestured, and the red-eyed vampires swarmed over the twelve sailors. They ripped and tore throats, arms, and legs and buried their dark snouts in the men, draining them dry with obscene sucking sounds.

Varlek stood before Brackenridge and studied his face for a moment. "Yes," he said, "right –" On the word "there," Varlek's hand whipped across Brackenridge's face with blinding speed and slashed his cheek from his jaw to his nose with a razor sharp fingernail.

"Should you live, Captain, every day you look into your mirror, you will be reminded of the meaning of true power." The vampire's dark tongue licked the blood from his nail. "Your blood tastes of hard tack and salt pork." He spat on the deck. "Not worth killing."

With that, Varlek strutted arrogantly across the deck and crossed the boarding plank to the Votrelec. Brackenridge tried to break free to pursue the vampire, to tear him to pieces with his bare hands, but the *trúdovi* held him fast. As the last of Varlek's crew left the Avenger, Sergi stood before Brackenridge. He shook his head sadly, and delivered a hammer blow to Brackenridge's brow with his huge fist that knocked him to the deck, where he lay as the bearded sailor left the ship, with the *trúdovi* behind him.

Brackenridge lay still for some time, dazed by the blow and by the horrors he'd seen. He raised himself to his elbows and dragged his body across the blood slick deck to a capstan that he used to haul himself to his feet. On shaky legs, he staggered to the rail to see the lights of the Votrelec disappearing into the mist, like balls of glowing wool.

He swore at that moment that if it cost him his life or his eternal soul, he would hunt down the monster and destroy him.

Like a man in a trance, he wandered about the Avenger, every moment revealing a fresh nightmare. A sailor torn in half lay on either side of the helm. One of his lieutenants sprawled over a water cask, but Brackenridge couldn't identify him. The man's face had been ripped off like a carnivale vizard, leaving his bloody skull exposed, its eyes staring in terror. The dead were hung like crimson ornaments from the rigging, dripping gore onto the deck.

The scene below decks was no better. Brackenridge stepped over bodies sprawled in the gangways and passages, necks broken, disemboweled, heads torn from their stumps and all cast aside like broken dolls. Then he saw Willie, the cabin boy, his freckled face, eyes closed and cherubic, and a yawning hole where his guts had been scooped out and left in a stinking pile beside him before he even knew to fear.

Brackenridge bent double and puked on the deck, his throat burning from bile and brandy. He sat down heavily, back against the bulkhead, breath coming in gulps and gasps. He cursed Varlek for letting him live and cursed himself for not slipping into the sweet embrace of madness.

I have lived one day too long, he thought, and another comes with the dawn. Vampires. He had heard of them, had felt a *frisson* at hearthside tales heard as a child on winter's nights, but no fable could match the absolute horror of reality. He racked his brain to recall the stories of his childhood. What destroys a vampire? Daylight. Silver. A wooden stake through the heart.

Brackenridge rose and stumbled back onto the topside deck. He pushed aside the corpse of a midshipman and opened the door to the carpenter's shed. He picked up a spoke shave and a piece of ash the length of his leg and the thickness of his wrist. He carried these to his cabin and pulled his chair away from the table. He wedged the ash pole between his boot heels and drew the two-handed tool toward him, scraping a looping sliver of the grey wood as he did.

Scrape. Another wooden curlicue fell to the floor. Scrape. Another, tapering the end of the pole slowly, but inexorably to the spike's point that would pierce Varlek's heart when next they met. In comparison, Captain Pettigrew's obsession was naught but a passing fancy.

LXX

Behind the barricade, the defenders were raw-nerved from hours of vigil, eyes wide and poised to spring at the first sign of the invaders. Inside the church, a different kind of vigil was taking place, prayers and rosaries among the islanders, the women, the elderly, and the children, huddled in the nave. The benches were taken outside to contribute to the barricade and the congregation sat on the floor, too close together to lie down.

Outside, Diego stood beside Cataldo, staring beyond the torchlight.

Cataldo rubbed his aching eyes with his fists. "I don't think they're coming."

"If they are, they will be coming soon. Another hour brings the sun."

As if a curtain had been drawn, the chatter of the night birds and the monkeys ceased.

"Look!" said Brio, pointing.

A lone figure approached.

All around him, Diego heard the click of cocking hammers.

"Tell the men not to fire unless I do, but be ready. This may be a trick, a diversion." Diego told Cataldo. "Pass the word."

The figure came into the circle of the firelight. Diego said, "Hold." The figure stood still and raised empty hands.

"Please, do not shoot me."

Cataldo said, "It's Sebastian de la Vega." The name rippled through the ranks of the defenders

"Armonia's chief?"

"Yes."

Father Beppo appeared at their side. "What is happening?"

"It's Sebastian," Cataldo said.

Sebastian walked slowly but purposefully into the light. He stopped thirty feet from the barricade.

"What is your message?" Cataldo demanded.

"My friends," he said. "I come to you with a message and an offer. Varlek the Master has come from the sea. To resist him will cause nothing but harm to you. Lay down your weapons and come out. Varlek has come, and he offers you peace, wealth, and prosperity if you will serve him. You will not be harmed if you submit."

"He sounds drugged," said Diego.

"Or in a trance." Cataldo shouted, "Sebastian, what is this peace, wealth and prosperity you offer?"

Sebastian droned, "Varlek the Master will nurture and protect you all if you serve him as ruler."

"Is this Varlek one of the people from that ship you were on? Is he the one who attacked us last night? We should lay down our arms and accept him as ruler? As conqueror, you mean. As despot. Would you have us become slaves?"

"Varlek will not allow you to come to harm if –"

"Not come to harm?" Christophe shouted. "I saw with my own eyes what was done to Esperanza. Men, women, slaughtered. They will do the same to us." Angry murmurs and curses rippled through the defenders. "You betray your own people!"

Sebastian shook his head. "No, no. Varlek will not allow –"

"Sebastian!" Jada burst from the doors of the church and would have tried to climb over the barricade if the men didn't stop her. She struggled as they held her back. "Sebastian!"

Hearing her voice, he stopped in mid-sentence. His eyes darted around the barricade looking for her. "Jada!" he cried, the trance broken. He took one step forward, then another, hesitant, as if struggling against a restraint. His arms moved as if her were swimming through the air. "Jada!"

From behind him, a shape came from the mist at a blurring speed. A hand caught Sebastian by the nape of his neck, lifted him off the ground, and hurled him over its shoulder. Shadowy figures rushed from the shadows and fell upon Sebastian, gorging themselves on his blood.

Jada screamed, and the men pulled her back from the barricade. "Get her inside the church." Cataldo snarled.

Varlek stood in the courtyard. His long black coat hung from him like folded wings. His face glowed in the torchlight. The vampire smiled, his fangs glinting in the flickering light. "It seems I must speak for myself. How disappointing. I had hoped that one of your own might more easily than I approach you and make you listen to reason."

His words seemed to swirl in the air around everyone's head, dart into one ear then another, echoing where there should be no echo. Diego heard the voice speaking in a melodic language he had never heard, and at the same time heard it inside his head in flawless Spanish. He looked at the men around him and all were rapt, fixed on the vampire's speech.

"Pike?" The mate turned to him, wide-eyed. "He's talking some gibberish, but I hear him in the King's English. What kind of trick is that?"

The vampire's eyes began to glow a dull red. Diego felt himself drawn into them, as if he were being pulled toward him inexorably. His hands lowered his musket and he felt it slipping from his nerveless fingers.

"You have seen what my minions can do. Esperanza?" He shrugged. "A necessary demonstration. We can besiege you day and night, and sooner or later, you will have to come out of that church. Resistance will do you no good. Sooner or later you will submit to me or die.

"Serve me. I can offer you wealth, prosperity, power – I can offer you eternal life."

"Blasphemy!" Father Beppo rushed to the front of the barricade, holding his crucifix over his head. "Look away from him! Cover your ears!" he shouted. "Be gone, demon! In the name of our savior Jesus Christ I order you to be gone!"

Varlek laughed. "You pathetic little man. You have no power over me."

Beppo threw the crucifix like a dagger, and it landed at the vampire's feet. Varlek hissed and stepped back, drawing the lapel of his coat over his face."

"Lies!" cried Beppo. "Lies! You see him quail before the sign of the cross."

Diego, shaken from his trance broke free from Varlek's eyes and raised his musket. As he pulled the trigger, one of the islanders still under Varlek's spell stepped between Diego and his target, knocking the muzzle aside and making the shot go wide. Others opened fire, sending a fusillade of silver shot and balls flying, but none of them touched Varlek. The vampire had vanished.

"Fools." The silken voice bounced from tree to tree and from the corners of the church to ring in every man's skull. "You think you, who have not lived one lifetime can destroy me, one who has lived so many? I will return tomorrow at sunset for your answer. Remember, there are many hours between nightfall and the dawn."

From inside the church came wailing and screams. Those inside had heard Varlek's words as well.

LXXI

Varlek stood on deck as the Votrelec dropped anchor in Armonia's bay. In a few moments he would retire once again to his coffin and take his rest. The British vessel had interrupted his plans. He would have taken Cuerpo Santo this night and been done with it, but he could not risk the self-righteous Englishmen joining forces with the islanders.

But there was always benefit to balance loss in life's scales. The Avenger was larger, faster, and had more firepower. The gunship would be a more effective vessel to raid and ravish other islands. Once the Exiles were secured, his crew would retrieve the British man-of-war and make her the flagship of his navy.

His would become a kingdom to rival all others, and once he ruled the sea, mortal kings would bow to him or fear his wrath. From the Exiles, he would strike at every island and port of the Atlantic. As the need for more of his soldiers grew, he would turn captives, some into vampires, some into *trúdovi*, all in his thrall.

Batteaux appeared at his side. "The girl, Marla; we no longer need her to coerce Sebastian. What shall I do with her?"

Varlek rubbed his chin. "Take her below with the others. I will enjoy her at my leisure. Right now I have other things to ponder."

From the east, he felt warmth, soon to be unbearable heat. The sun was about to rise. With the sunset would come victory, a kingdom, and glory. He raised the coffin's lid and gazed on the beauty of the sleeping Francine. He had given his word to Batteaux in exchange for his faithful service that Francine would remain untouched, and thus far, Batteaux had not failed him. But, thought, Varlek, humans are fallible. The day would come when Batteaux would falter, and Francine would rule beside him as his queen.

Her lot would not be as one of the Anointed. They were little more than red eyed savages lusting for blood, doing his bidding. Francine would become an elite entity, a minor deity like himself to rule forever. Someday, they would rule the world. He climbed into the coffin and pulled the lid closed. To sleep, he thought, perchance to dream…

LXXII

Diego stood by the forge as Tomás heaped charcoal into the fire pit. He looked to the chest of silver that stood more than half empty beside him. The panic firing of the night before had depleted their stock of silver musket balls and shot, and the remaining silver would leave them with even less than they had the night before.

He could not blame the islander who deflected his aim. Varlek had them all in a state of confusion. But Diego was certain that he would have put a silver ball through the vampire's heart and perhaps ended the whole business. Yet, without their leader's restraining hand, who knew what the bestial white-eyes and the even more deadly vampires might do.

Varlek's scheme, to create an island kingdom for himself was a devilishly clever one. He would rule through fear. Once conquered, who among the islanders could oppose him and live to do anything about it?

And how long would they maintain their resolve? All in the church heard Varlek's words, and already some of them and even some of the men at the barricades are arguing that perhaps surrender would be the lesser of evils.

The priest had told him that Varlek had made his army of vampires by biting them and then sharing his blood, and as their creator, he commanded them. But old Beppo knew nothing about the white-eyed fiends that served Varlek, what they were, how they were made, and how they were controlled.

He did know that they could be killed; he had seen the proof in the church yard. Killed? They were perhaps dead already and brought back through some hellish sorcery; Beppo thought so. But crushing their skulls or taking off their heads laid them low.

Tomás, stripped to the waist, pulled the handle of the bellows, breathing life into the coals. His thick muscles rippled under his already sweat-slick skin. Outside the forge, Diego saw Raoul coming down the path. He was carrying a sack.

"What is it, Raoul?"

"Father Beppo went among the men and women and gathered jewelry, coins, anything made of silver for your weapons." He opened the bag and inside it, Diego saw an array of rings, hair combs, pins, and coins. He also saw a silver crucifix, a span long.

He turned it over in his hands. "It seems a sacrilege to melt this down."

"Father Beppo said that the Savior would understand."

"Thank you, Raoul. We will use these gifts well."

As Raoul walked away, Diego turned the crucifix over in his hands, ran his thumb over its length. When Tomás poured the silver into the crucible, Diego held the crucifix back.

He searched through the tools on Tomás's workbench, picked up a hammer, and said, "I need a file."

While Tomás and Ortega cast the balls, Diego set about working on the crucifix. From the feet of the figura, about the length of his forefinger, Diego hammered the beam of the cross, flattening it and widening it to about half its thickness and twice its width. He then drew the file along its sides, tapering the tip to a point, and working its edges front and back.

He had seen one before, a crucifix with a deadly blade, in the hands of a Trinidadian assassin called the Dark Angel. He had been sent to kill Diego by the vengeful brother of a privateer Diego had killed in battle. The murderer had come to the pirates' table at the Trebuchet, a tavern near the docks, disguised as a monk and saying he had a message for the Hand.

"Is he among you?" The holy man looked out of place in such a den of iniquity, his hood down, exposing his tonsure. Bare feet in simple strap sandals showed below the hem of his brown, coarse-spun robe.

Brio spoke up. "That would be me, *Padre*."

The monk nodded. "Very good."

"And whose lips are the source of this message?"

"It is a delicate matter, an affair *du coeur*. Bend an ear to me, Captain, and I shall tell all."

When Brio leaned forward in his chair, the Dark Angel threw the table over, blocking Brio's friends and seized the wooden crucifix by its upper part. He pulled it away to reveal the wicked dagger hidden in the upright of the cross.

Diego swung his mug and clubbed the Angel across his jaw. The assassin staggered back, giving Diego time to rise and pull a blade of his own.

His men reached for pistols and knives, but he waved them back. "No, this is my fight."

People scattered, upsetting chairs and spilling drinks. They retreated to the fringes of the room, eager to stay out of harm's way but as eager to see harm done. None dared interfere.

Diego and the Angel circled each other, each looking for an opening. The Angel cut the braided cord that held the robe closed with one slash, testimony to the sharpness of the edge. The robe fell open, and Diego saw the bare-chested Angel wore leather breeches that came to his shins.

The Angel moved like a dancer, twisting and turning, not only to evade Diego's thrusts and slashes but to allow the billowing robe to confuse and conceal. He held the hem by his free hand like a bull fighter would a cape and swirled it between himself and Diego's knife.

The Angel took a step forward and feinted at Diego's belly. When Diego lowered his arm to block the thrust, the Angel turned its arc upward, narrowly missing his throat and slashing Diego's cheek.

The assassin laughed. "You have spent too many hours hacking with a cutlass, lo Mano. You lack the *délicatesse* to wield a finer blade." He took another step forward, and Diego, instead of counter thrusting, threw his dagger downward, piercing the Angel's sandaled foot and pinning it to the floor.

The Angel screamed and swung his knife hand, but Diego stepped in and caught the arm under his own. He twisted his torso and heard the Dark Angel's bones crack at the elbow. He drove a fist into the Dark Angel's throat, and the would-be killer fell backward to the floor, knee bent, his foot still pinned by the Hand's knife.

"It was not personal," the Angel coughed, choking on blood. "Just business."

Diego pulled his dagger from the assassin's foot and plunged it through his heart. "No, nothing personal. Nothing at all."

In Tomás's forge Diego carefully filed the sides of the flattened metal, shaping and honing. He ran his thumb across the edge of his newly fashioned weapon. The silver was too soft a metal to hold an edge long, but sharp once would be enough.

LXXIII

Christophe looked around nervously, fingering the hammer of his pistol. The noon heat was oppressive, but he felt a chill nonetheless. The forest around the town was too quiet for his liking. He and two others stood guard as a group of islanders drew water from a well at the town's edge to replenish the supply in the church. He had volunteered to go with them because he had no wife or children.

The people huddled inside were restless and although aware of the peril that lay outside the church walls, numb to it from exhaustion and anticipation. Sebastian's appearance the previous night followed by that of the vampire Varlek, sparked dissension among the islanders. As many seemed willing to surrender and submit, believing the promise of peace and prosperity as were determined to fight to the death to remain free. The story that Varlek was fired upon without consequence led to rumors that he could not die, which led to two ways of thinking; one, the belief that Varlek could indeed impart immortality, and the other the belief that resisting him was indeed futile, if he and his minions could not be killed.

Father Beppo insisted otherwise. He knew much that the common man did not, but Varlek's appearance dealt a blow to the priest's support and credibility.

"We are filling the last barrel," Phillipe said, wiping the sweat from his brow with a kerchief.

"Good. The sooner we are away from here and back inside the church, the better." Parties had been sent out earlier in the day to bring in food and reported no sign of the white-eyed monsters or of their human masters. Christophe wanted to believe that they were gone, but in his heart, he knew that was not true.

The men struggled with the heavy barrel, large enough to hold four men, three of them rolling it up the plank into the back of the cart. The ox suddenly raised its head, nostrils flaring. It tossed its head from side to side and began snorting.

Christophe read the signs. "Hurry. Get it on the wagon." He tucked his pistol into his belt and ran to help push the heavy cask up the ramp. As he put his shoulder to the barrel, he caught a glimpse of motion from the ferns to his right. *Trúdovi*, at least six of them, burst from the thick green, snarling and baring their rotten teeth. Pistols were fired. Men screamed in terror and in pain.

An islander swung an axe, shattering the knee of one of the attackers and almost cutting through. The *trúdovi's* leg buckled and it fell. As the man with the axe stepped in to deal a killing blow to the monster's head, the *trúdovi*, not slowed at all by what would be a mortal wound in a human, scuttled forward on three limbs and grabbed him by the knees, pulling itself up the screaming man's torso, and sank its teeth in his shoulder.

Christophe reached for his pistol but the hammer caught in his belt. One of the attackers was upon him before he could work it loose. The ox, panicked by the creatures, lumbered forward, and two of the barrels rolled backward to tumble off the cart. One of them landed on the back of a *trúdovi* who was gouging at Christophe, claws digging into his throat. The heavy barrel broke the creature's spine but did not kill it. It lay pinned under the cask, its hellish mewling filling Christophe's ears as he fought with a forearm to keep the snapping fangs of his opponent out of reach.

The head, he thought, destroy the head. He gave a shove that pushed the *trúdovi's* weight from his chest for a second, and he pulled the pistol free. The creature twisted at him again, and he shoved the muzzle of the flintlock into its gaping mouth. Christophe closed his eyes and prayed as he pulled the trigger.

The back of the *trúdovi's* head exploded in a spray of dark gore and the creature rolled off him. He rose to a crouch only to have another leap on his back, its talons digging into his shoulders. He shoved to his feet and reared backward, and he felt bones crack as he smashed the gaunt body against the wagon. Beside him Roberto was pounding the head of his attacker with a sharp edged rock. He raised it with both hands for the *coup de gras*, and another of the white eyed devils dove at him and knocked him aside.

Christophe felt a blaze of pain, and looked down at his chest where the barb of a pike had burst through his shirt. He fell to his knees and groped at the pike as if he could pull it through him and out of his chest. Then he felt a foot at his back and the *trúdovi* pulled it free to impale him again.

All around him were dying, and as his eyes dimmed, Christophe saw a spectacled man with a ginger beard step from the cover of the forest. He barked an order to the *trúdovi*, and two of them rolled the heavy cask away from their comrade. The spectacled man studied the broken-backed creature and drew his pistol. With no more expression than if he were shooting a horse with a broken leg, he put a ball through the *trúdovi's* skull.

The *trúdovi*, finshed with their killing, were rolling the casks of water onto the wagon, while two of them held the ox by its yoke. Despite the beast's stomping and bucking, the pair held the ox in check.

They were there, watching the whole time, Christophe thought, waiting for us to draw the water for them so they wouldn't have to do it for themselves.

Batteaux saw Christophe staring at him and said something to one of the *trúdovi*. The white-eyed killer picked up Roberto's stone and skulked toward Christophe. It raised the stone above its head. Blackness.

LXXIV

Diego stood in the churchyard where Father Beppo, Cataldo, and others of the island's men stood in a group.

"They have been gone too long," muttered Raoul. "Christophe and the others should have returned by now."

"And we are nearly out of water," said Rudolfo, another of the men. "We will die of thirst before the attackers kill us."

"If what the *Padre* tells us is so, perhaps it might be a better death."

Rudolfo spat. "You are alone. You have no wife, no children who are suffering." He turned his eyes to the casks of blessed water.

"Don't even think of taking the holy water," Diego said. "It is a weapon. Would you eat our gunpowder too?"

"And you," Rudolfo snarled, "a pirate, a killer, a reaver. We should listen to you? You brought this plague upon us." He started toward Diego, fists raised. Diego's men closed around him, and Rudolfo's friends stepped behind him.

"Enough of this," Father Beppo snapped. "This man has brought his crew to stand with us against the evil. He has armed you and given up his treasure to melt down for balls to fire in the muskets he has brought, with powder that he has brought. We need to stand together, not fight among ourselves. Me must—"

Gunshots came from the front of the church. Cataldo and Diego rushed ahead of the group to find Pike and a handful of others aiming muskets over the barricade. "Out there in the clearing," he said, pointing. Diego followed his gesture and saw a burlap sack lying halfway between the trees and the barricade.

"One of those raggedy white-eyed bastards broke from the brush and threw the sack. We might have hit him; I don't know for sure."

"If you didn't hit him in the head, you wasted your powder," Cataldo said.

"What do you think, Diego?" Brio said. "Is it a trick to lure us out to retrieve the bag?"

"Could be. If one of us goes out there to retrieve it, he'd be an easy target for a musket ball. Cataldo said that he spoke to humans on the Votrelec. Just because the white-eyes don't use weapons, we can't assume that others in their group don't." He thought for a moment then said, "With all the tools we brought for weapons, did we bring a *rezón*?"

"I'm sure we did. I'll find it." Brio hurried away.

"And I'll need a length of rope."

Brio returned carrying a three-barbed hook with a shaft as long as his forearm. Diego knotted the rope through the eye at its base. "Stand away," he said. He swung the hook in a circle beside him for momentum and let it fly, pulling he rope behind it." The *rezón* fell a few feet short of the sack. "Damn." He tried again and this time the grapnel landed a few feet past the sack but too far to the right to be of use. The third time, it landed a few feet behind the bag, the rope trailing over it. He slowly pulled at the rope and when one of the tines of the *rezón*, pierced the sack, he tugged at the rope sharply to set the hook in the coarse fabric. He tugged again and the sack moved. "Got it."

Diego pulled the rope in hand over hand, dragging the bag across the packed earth, slowly so as to not dislodge the hook. When it reached the barricade, one of the crewmen scrambled like a monkey over the sharp spikes of the abatis. Diego held his breath, expecting a gunshot any second, but none came. The crewman hurled the sack over the barricade and it landed with a thump at Diego's feet. He scrambled back inside, and the men gathered around to see what was in the sack.

Diego lifted the sack. It was heavy and bulged with shapes like coconuts. He slit the side open and the sack emptied its contents, human heads, among them Christophe's.

The men began murmuring, some of them crossing themselves. "Well," said Cataldo. "I suppose that means we won't be getting fresh water."

"Listen to me," Diego snapped. "All of you. Not a word of this to anyone. Do you understand? We don't want to cause panic." Heads nodded in agreement. He turned to one of the islanders. "Bring the priest."

By the time Father Beppo came, Diego had wrapped the heads in the burlap. He handed the priest the bundle. "These were brave men, *Padre*. Please give them the honor they deserve."

Beppo opened a corner of the burlap and when saw what was inside, he flinched and sadly shook his head. "It will be done."

"What do we do now, Diego?" said Pike.

"We do what I should have done at the outset. We bring the Belladonna to the fight. Cataldo, you saw the Votrelec. How many guns?"

"I didn't count them. I had other things on my mind at the time, but a good number. Twelve to the side, at least."

"Were the ports open or closed?"

"Closed. We posed no threat. But there's no surety that every port had a

... he tugged at the rope sharply to set the hook in the coarse fabric.

cannon under its hatch, either."

"That's true, but we have to assume the worst. Overland will take too long. I'll take men in one of your boats and bring the Belladonna around the island. The vampires have to sleep in their native soil. In coffins. Is that not so, *Padre*?

Father Beppo nodded. "From all I have read, yes. It is so."

"I'm betting that those coffins are on the Votrelec, and to bring his full force to battle, Varlek must bring the ship into the harbor. I want to bring the Belladonna into play to harass the Votrelec while she's anchored and putting her full force ashore."

"Take my sloop, the Sirena." said Cataldo. "But what if the Votrelec spots you before you return? You can't fight or run with a short crew."

"It's a chance I have to take. Whatever we do it should be in daylight." He turned to Beppo. "*Padre*, pray for us. We need all the help we can get. Luck, skill, and courage may not be enough."

Beppo reached into his robe and pulled out a crucifix on a finely wrought chain. "Take this." Diego held out his hand and the priest put it in his palm and closed his fingers over it. "You'll find it a stronger weapon than any sword or gun."

LXXV

Diego and eight men including Brio and Pike armed themselves with extra pistols and set off for the docks. The town, which was ordinarily bustling, lay silent as if holding its breath. The pirates expected an attack around every corner of the winding streets and moved with caution. Most unnerving were the windows, each one a dark hole in the noonday sun, each hiding a potential peril.

Brio stood still and raised a hand. "Listen. Birds, and monkeys, but they're too far away."

"That means that the invaders are close by. Keep a sharp watch."

The marketplace was desolate, the stalls and the bins stripped of everything edible to feed the refugees in the church. "There should be gulls," said Pike, "monkeys, rats to gnaw on the bones."

"Like a sinking ship, eh?" said Brio. No one laughed at the joke. It was as if the entire town had died, and the island soon to follow. Past the market, the pirates saw the pilings and timbers of the docks. The boats bobbed at their moorings, the only thing moving in the oppressive heat.

Cataldo's sloop, one of the larger boats lay near the end of the dock that projected into the harbor's cove.

"They look untouched," said Pike. "I'd've put a hole in every one of 'em. Keep people from sailing away."

"That's not the plan," Diego said. "Varlek doesn't want to destroy these people. Once the siege ends, he wants their lives to go on as they were, but under his thumb. They are fishermen, farmers; destroy their means of livelihood and you breed rebellion. He promises them peace and prosperity. He wants them relatively happy, not resentful. Destroy their boats, their barns, their crops, and he would have to kill every one of them, and what is a king without subjects?"

"Or a god without worshippers?" said Brio. "Nothing."

"Well put." Diego nodded with resolution. "Let's go. Be ready."

They cautiously moved forward onto the dock, realizing they had no avenue of escape but to jump into the sea, which lapped at the pilings with undisturbed regularity. The business of men and monsters meant nothing to the pulsing waves.

"I have an idea," said Donald. "Let's take the first boat at hand and get out into the water, get to Cataldo's sloop that way."

Diego raised his hand to halt. "Not a bad idea." A longboat lay to their left, oars in the bow. "That one. Climb in."

Half were in the boat when a chorus of snarls erupted from the middle of the pier. *Trúdovi* erupted from the bows of boats tethered at the pilings. They dropped from the furled sails of others, landing on the planking or splashing into the water.

"Hurry," Diego shouted. "Jump into the boat." He swung his cutlass and cut the mooring rope then put his shoulder to the piling and shoved the longboat away from the dock. Donald leapt into the stern, and cried out in pain. He had broken his shin on the thwart. Robbie, the last man on the dock, missed the boat and splashed into the water. Brio held out his hand, but as Robbie reached for it, a *trúdovi* bobbed out of the sea and wrapped its arms around him, pulling him under.

In a moment, the sea was alive with the white-eyed minions as they dove from the dock and from the ships in pursuit of the pirates. One tried to climb into the stern as Pike fitted oars into the locks and began to pull with all the strength he could muster. Diego swung his cutlass backhand and the monster's head fell from its body, which then topped backward into the water.

Taloned hands curved over the gunwale and a hideous head appeared. The *trúdovi* had pulled itself halfway into the boat when Brio brought an axe down across the clutching fingers of one hand, then the other.

More oars were set, and the boat pulled away from the swimming horde. Brio took the tiller. "To the sloop, Captain?"

Diego shielded his eyes and saw movement on deck. A huge bearded man stood up and bellowed orders in a strange guttural tongue. Behind them, the *trúdovi* still swam in pursuit. The pirates rowed desperately, and soon were almost into the open sea. Diego looked back and his heart sank. The sloop was slipping away from the dock, and its sail was spreading with the wind. They could never outrun her. Soon they would be overtaken, and then they would fight and likely die. "Pull," Diego shouted, "into the wind. Make for the reef. The tide's out, and if luck is with us, we'll glide right over and he won't."

LXXVI

At the helm of the sloop, Sergi grinned broadly. Varlek's plan did not work exactly, but it was effective nonetheless with Sergi's addition to it. The pirates did not pass the middle of the dock where they would be trapped and surrounded by *trúdovi*, but Sergi's idea of being ready to sail in pursuit no matter which vessel the escapees might choose proved correct. Varlek would reward him well for this victory.

Pescu removed his spectacles and put the telescope to his eye. "Those are no island fishermen. They're armed to their chaps. They look like buccaneers. They'll put up a hard fight."

"They'll never have the chance."

Already the sloop was gaining on the longboat, and no matter how hard the sailors rowed, their efforts were useless. Sergi's only regret was that the fishing boat had no cannon on its deck. They were in the open water now, and he was tacking against the wind. In moments he would overtake them, and splinter their boat to kindling.

The sloop rose with a swell and as it sidled into the trough a sudden impact threw the *trúdovi* to the deck. Had Sergi not been gripping the wheel, he too would have fallen. Pescu, standing at the rail, was pitched overboard.

Sergi roared and smashed his fist against the wheel. They had tricked him. The longboat was pulling away, and a man in the stern stood in the boat and bared his buttocks in derision.

"Throw me a line," Pescu shouted, treading water near the bow.

Sergi threw a rope over the side and Pescu swam toward it. He grabbed the rope at the same instant Sergi saw the fin slicing the water behind him. With a mighty effort, Sergi yanked at the rope and Pescu was halfway out of the water when the shark rose from the waves and its ugly maw closed around Pescu's waist.

Sergi let go of the rope. No one wins a tug of war with a shark.

LXXVII

The pirates looked back to see the sloop broken on the reef. "We got away from them, but we still have to get to the Belladonna," Brio said.

"We can't go back for another boat. Those monsters will be waiting, so let's start rowing."

Steering by the sun, the pirates pulled at the oars, exhausted from battle and lack of sleep. Donald lay in the stern, his leg splinted with a musket. Nearly an hour had passed, when he sat up and cried out, "A ship!"

Diego shielded his eyes. He had not seen it before because the sails were furled, only masts on the horizon.

"Who is she, Captain?" one of the men said.

"I can't say, but for all the world she looks like the Avenger in her build."

Brio pulled a collapsing spyglass from his pouch. "Here, Diego, have a look."

The lens brought the ship into clearer focus. "I see the bowsprit, the lady with the sword." The ship was definitely their nemesis. "It is the Avenger. I'm certain of it."

"Then let's run before one of her crew sees us."

"Wait," Diego said. He handed the glass to Pike. "Something's not right. Tell me what you see."

Pike studied the ship for a full minute before saying, "I see gulls. They're all over the ship, no men. Also, she seems to be lying idle, dead in the water."

"If all were right, she'd be at full sail looking for the Belladonna. This is curious."

"Do you think it's a trick?"

"Doubtful. Unless the whole crew is hiding in the hold, those gulls wouldn't be there. She looks to be drifting. Something is wrong on board." Diego thought for a moment then said, "I say we go to her and find out what it is."

"Captain, they'll shoot you on sight."

"Not if we look like islanders. Put your weapons in the bow." He turned to Pike. "Give me your shirt." Pike stripped off his shirt and Diego tied it to an oar as a truce flag. He braced it in the bow and said, "Pull for the Avenger, boys, and let's hope our luck holds."

LXXVIII

On the Avenger, Brackenridge sat on the poop deck, head in his hands. His bloody uniform coat lay in a crumpled heap beside him. The Avenger had drifted idly all night, and though he could see an island in the distance, he had no idea which one it might be. He would have dropped anchor, but he feared that he would not be able to work the winch to raise it again by himself.

The gulls covered the corpses of his crew in an undulating blanket of white like that he'd seen on Esperanza. He'd run screaming at the defiling birds, but as soon as they lifted away from one pile of bodies, they settled again on another. Like bailing out the sea with a bucket, he thought, and he resigned himself to the fact that like the Book of Revelation, the carrion birds were invited to the feast.

Something caught his eye across the water. A flutter of white bobbed in the waves. In a moment he could see a longboat with a group of men pulling oars in the open sea. The white was a flag of truce.

Who are they? He thought. Did the vampires lay waste to another ship? He stood and unbuttoned his waistcoat. He waved it over his head back and forth, acknowledging the boat. Whoever they are, he thought, they are not from Varlek, and their help is welcome.

"Captain," said Brio, "A man on deck, waving a cloth."

Diego raised the glass to his eye. "*Si*, and only one. He handed the glass to Donald. "Keep watch for others," he said and went back to his oar. In half an hour, the longboat was alongside the Avenger.

"Do you smell it, Captain?" Brio said.

"I do. Carrion, and strong."

"Ahoy, aboard," called Pike in his best English accent. A head appeared over the railing above, followed by the barrel of a blunderbuss.

"Easy, mate," Pike said. "Don't shoot us. Our ship was sunk. We barely escaped with our lives."

Brackenridge cocked the hammer. "Are you with Varlek?"

Diego recognized the eyes of madness and seized the opportunity. "No, my friend. He is the one who sank our ship, he and his monsters. We barely escaped alive." Diego pulled the *Padre's* crucifix from his shirt and held it in his fist. "Could I hold this in the light of day if I were one of his creatures?"

Indecision flickered in Brackenridge's eyes. Finally, the prospect of no longer being alone won out. "No, you're not of Varlek's crew; come aboard." He threw a ladder over the side and a rope to tie their boat.

Diego and his men climbed aboard, all but Donald, and stood in stunned silence at the heaps of corpses covered with squawking, pecking birds. The stench of corruption stung their nostrils.

"Your crew?" Diego said. He saw the haunted look on the Englishman's face.

"Aye," Brackenridge answered, nodding. "Dead to the last man."

"Killed by Varlek and his creatures?"

Brackenridge nodded. "You've seen them?"

"And fought them," Diego replied.

"And who might you be?" Pike said.

"Lieutenant William Brackenridge, acting captain of His Majesty's Ship the Avenger."

"Acting captain? And where is Pettigrew?"

Brackenridge's head snapped up, shaken from his fog. "You knew the Captain?"

"We've never met, truth be told, but I'd say we knew each other well enough. I am Diego lo Mano, Captain of the Belladonna."

"You." Brackenridge's eyes darted around searching for the blunderbuss, but it was out of reach. Pike stepped between him and the weapon. Brackenridge's eyes widened. He began to draw his sword, but Diego's men seized his arms and pinned them to his sides. "You're the reason for all this." He swung his chin, indicating the dead on the deck. "You led us into this hell."

"I could as easily say you drove us into it. My ship and crew are in the same peril." Diego looked over the bodies on the deck. ""Pettigrew is among these?"

"No. He was killed by a falling spar a few nights ago when the mast was struck by lightning."

"And you assumed command?"

"I succeeded the Captain."

"Whatever word suits you, Brackenridge, it is no matter." Diego drew the Englishman's sword and handed it to Brio. He raised his hands and turned around. "As you see, I too am unarmed. Let us sit down and talk like sensible men."" He looked around the deck. "Perhaps out of the sun and out of this stench."

"I have no choice, do I?"

Diego nodded to his men, who released Brackenridge. "We have an injured man who needs attention." He turned to Brio. "Bring Donald aboard."

Brackenridge led Diego and Pike to his cabin. The first thing Diego noticed was a pile of wood shavings on the floor. His eyes searched the room, and he saw the wooden stake, sharpened to a needle point, standing in a corner. He picked it up and tested the tip with his thumb. "Your handiwork?"

Brackenridge took the stake from Diego, and Pike's hand dropped to his pistol. Diego raised a hand for his mate to stand down.

Brackenridge turned the sharpened pole in his hands, studying it. "What do you know of vampires?"

"Only a handful of legends and what Father Beppo, the priest on Cuerpo Santo has told us, which seems little more credible."

"Stories I heard as a boy had it that a vampire could be killed by a stake through his heart."

"So you fashioned this for Varlek?"

"Aye, and when next we meet, I'll do for him like he did for my crew."

Diego pulled a chair to the table and sat. Pike stood to the side, watchful for any surprise from the Englishman. "May I?" Diego said, indicating the decanter of brandy. Not waiting for a reply, he poured two glasses and pushed one toward Brackenridge, who finally sat, laying the stake on the table. He drank the brandy at a single pull, coughed, and began to speak.

"Searching for you island by island, we found an entire population slain."

"Esperanza," Diego said, recalling Christophe's account. "One of the islanders also found the dead and told us about it."

"We buried the dead and set out to find you, thinking you and your crew were responsible."

"You know now that we were not."

Brackenridge nodded slowly. "I know now that it was Varlek's minions."

He recounted spotting the Votrelec and giving chase, and the bearded man throwing the children overboard.

"The bearded man, a hulking brute?"

"Yes. He was a big as two of me. A Russian by all appearances."

Diego said, "The same man pursued us when we left Cuerpo Santo's harbor. We left him stranded on a reef."

Brackenridge's eyes blazed. "If I had my crew, I'd hunt him down and blast him out of the water. They came in the night and the attack was so savage and overwhelming that my men had no chance to defend themselves. Most were killed in their sleep."

Diego sat for a few moments, silently he raised his head. "Pike, call Brio in here. We won't have enough time to bring the Belladonna to the fight, but the Avenger may serve."

Brackenridge stared. "Varlek killed my crew to prevent the Avenger from attacking. What can a dead ship do?"

"In the right hands, more than you may think, Brackenridge. More than you may think. The *Padre* told us that Varlek must rest in his coffin during the day. I'm betting that coffin is on board the Votrelec and if we destroy the ship, he'll be cut off from it and perhaps vulnerable."

"Destroy it? How?"

"How many guns to a side does the Avenger carry?"

"Twenty-two."

"Thirty-two pounders?"

"Twenty-fours."

"They should do for what I have in mind. We don't have enough hands for full sail, but we can surely harness a little wind to push us to the island. The vampires will attack the church on Cuerpo Santo tonight. Varlek as much as said so and the ship will have to anchor in the island's harbor to put Varlek's force ashore. That will leave few on the ship. Bottled up in the harbor, they will make a fine target."

"But–" At that moment, Pike returned with Brio.

"This is my helmsman. He is a sorcerer at the wheel. This is what I hope to do..."

LXXIX

"They are not coming back." Ramon Fiero muttered, pacing in the churchyard. "Those pirates have run for their lives and left us all to be slaughtered."

One of Diego's men, a swarthy sailor named Panzo told him. "The Hand fears nothing. He gave his word, not just to you and the priest but to us, his crew. If he does not return, it is because he has given his life."

"Oh, the Hand, the Hand!" Ramon sneered. "You think he cares a whit for a pack of scurvy dogs like you? He'll sail away and buy another crew just like you while your corpses rot in tomorrow's sun." Ramon grabbed at his crotch. "That for you and your rat turd friends."

"You – " Panzo drew his dagger and started toward Ramon, but Mobuti, the African giant, stepped between them.

"No, little brother," the big man said in a voice that vibrated in Panzo's chest. He closed his hand on the pirate's wrist, a hand that could have easily crushed the smaller man's bones. "Not here, not now. We have real enemies to fight, not each other."

"Prove to me you aren't cowards," Ramon jeered. "Don't fight from behind the barricade, go stand out front and meet the enemy like the brave men you claim—" Ramon was yanked off his feet from behind and thrown across the churchyard to land in Father Beppo's garden.

Cataldo stood over him, fists clenched. "Maybe you'd like to go out there, Ramon. If you make any more trouble, I'll throw you over the abatis myself. Or maybe I'll tether you outside like a goat as bait."

Ramon shook his head, wide-eyed. "No–no!"

"All of you," Cataldo shouted, "concern yourselves with who is here, not who isn't, who will stand beside you now and fight back to back with you. Enough of this." He glared a last time at Ramon and strode off before his temper got the best of him.

The nave of the church was sweltering between the tropical sun and the body heat of the masses huddled inside. Shoulder to shoulder, the frail, the women, and the children could not fall down because there was nowhere for them to fall. Two of the elderly, one man and one woman, had succumbed to the heat, and were now lying in the churchyard.

It would be hours before the sun sank low in the sky and the heat would ease, but with the setting of the sun would come Varlek. Every soul in the church had heard the vampire's offer and his warning, and as many wanted to surrender as wanted to fight, if for no other reason than to end their suffering.

Beppo walked among them, placing a hand of blessing on the foreheads of the children, a reassuring hand on the shoulders of their mothers, and the touch of comfort on the wizened faces of the old.

"*Padre*," one of them said, "when will it end?"

"Soon," the priest said. He was certain it would end soon, but not how.

LXXX

Batteaux stood at the helm of one of the fishing boats from Cuerpo Santo's harbor, watching as Sergi and his crew of *trúdovi* came on board. Sergi's mistake had wasted valuable time in preparation for the night's assault on the church. Varlek ordered him to be ready to attack with all the forces they had and overrun the islanders to bring them to heel. That meant bringing all the *trúdovi* and all of the "Anointed" onto the Votrelec and delivering them into Cuerpo Santo's harbor. The men who escaped could not go far in an open boat. What were they thinking?

Sergi stood beside him. "That is all."

"Varlek will be displeased at the loss of Pescu."

"It is a risk we all run. Take us back to the Votrelec."

LXXXI

Diego's first inclination was to throw the corpses of the Englishmen over the side and purge the Avenger of their putrefaction, but even in death the ship's crew could yet serve a purpose. The rest of the afternoon, Brackenridge, Diego, and his men would work at preparing the port side guns with rum-soaked kerchiefs over their noses and mouths. Most of the cannons they loaded with twenty-four pound balls, but a few were set with fire arrows, barbed projectiles dragging flaming oil soaked cloth behind them to set the sails and rigging ablaze.

They dragged the heavy guns into position and aimed most of them not to rake the bow of their target but to concentrate on one area of the hull. Brackenridge argued against that, reminding Diego that there were children on board and perhaps other prisoners who might die should the Votrelec sink. Diego stifled the argument with a simple question: having seen Varlek's thralls and his vampires at work, which death would the Englishman prefer for them? Should they die, a clean, natural death would be better.

"We cannot man all of the port side cannons with only a half dozen men," Diego said, "but we can set one master fuse to ignite those leading to each of the guns. They should all fire in less than a minute and do enough damage that we will cripple the Votrelec if not sink her."

The second part of Diego's plan was to lash every musket and pistol on the ship to the port railing, all primed and loaded, and to tie the body of one of the slain crewmen behind each. The pirates could run down the line firing one musket after another. There was no knowing how many humans were on board, but any damage their gunfire could do was a help. And the corpses at the railing would give the illusion of a live crew on the ship.

The rest was up to Brio. His skill as a helmsman would be sorely tried to make the plan work. "Is he able to do this?" Brackenridge asked.

"If any man alive can do it, he can."

The plan was bold. With as little sail as possible, steer the Avenger toward Cuerpo Santo and slip into the harbor while the crew of the Votrelec was preoccupied with the attack on the church. The Avenger would come within range of the Votrelec under cover of darkness – the vampires could not attack before sundown – and open fire. Diego was counting on the evening mist that often shrouded the islands to mask their approach.

"Do you think it'll work, Diego?" Pike said, wiping sweat from his brow with the back of his hand.

"I can only hope, my friend, but a slim chance is better than none at all."

LXXXII

The Votrelec lay at anchor in Armonia's harbor. Batteaux had only to take the *trúdovi* on board and wait for sunset when the Anointed would climb from their coffins. Varlek planned to make a great show of sailing the Votrelec into Cuerpo Santo's harbor with *trúdovi* in the rigging and crimson-eyed vampires lining the rail. The people cowering inside the church would not see their approach, but their lookouts would, and report the horrors that the ship brought.

"Let them see the force that I bring, and they will quake with terror. They will kneel before me rather than lose their miserable lives."

"They have resisted until now," Batteaux had pointed out, and Varlek said, "Their leaders have to make a show of resistance, have to make their people believe they have tried yet have no option but to yield to a superior force, so that even under my thumb they will keep their authority and some limited power of their own. They will bend the knee."

That had been the case before when they had taken an island or a town, then laid waste to man, woman and child, making the strongest part of Varlek's cadre of Anointed while others he made into *trúdovi* to replace those that had been damaged in battle or simply rotted away. This time, Varlek wanted more. Batteaux admitted to himself that the scheme, as mad as it seemed, could very well give Varlek the result he wanted. If it did, Batteaux hoped it would satisfy him and he would free Francine from his grip.

These islands are a paradise, Batteaux thought, and we are the serpents in Eden.

LXXXIII

"You know," said Cataldo, "this Varlek could destroy us all by simply waiting to act while we're bottled up in here. If he waits another day, half of us will die of thirst."

Vargas crouched in the shade of the abatis and mopped the sweat from his brow with a kerchief. "The vampire said he would return tonight. I believe that he will."

"And do you think the Hand will return as well?"

"He said that he will, and I believe him also."

Cataldo laughed. "You have great faith in a pirate who is as surely damned as I am, a faith as strong as the *Padre's*, I'll wager."

"You would do well to cultivate one like it of your own." Father Beppo said from behind him. "Faith, we are told by the apostle, is 'the assured expectation of things hoped for.'"

Cataldo turned and stared boldly into Beppo's eyes. "The only assurance

I see is the axe in my fist, *Padre*, begging your pardon. I do not expect legions of angels to swoop in and rescue us."

"Nor do I, Cataldo. Salvation must come from within as well as from without. If we do our part, the Savior will do his."

As the priest walked away, Cataldo said, "But I'd still like to scoop a draught from one of those barrels of holy water, before I die of thirst." The sound of crying children drifted from inside the church. "I wish their mothers would hush them."

Vargas swatted away a mosquito the size of a hummingbird. "They give us a reason beyond our own lives to fight. Do you have children of your own?"

Cataldo shook his head. "My wife lost three in childbirth. You?"

"Four in Madrid; one of them I have never seen. If you had children of your own, you would think differently, Cataldo. I fight for my own life, I fight for the lives of the people of this island, and I also fight for the lives of my children. Father Beppo is right. Unchecked, this evil will spread, until one day it lands on the shores of Spain and knocks at my woman's door. If we can halt it here and now, they will be safe."

Cataldo frowned and looked away. To such reasoning, he could make no answer.

LXXXIV

On the Avenger, Brackenridge labored with the pirates to ready the port side guns. *Contingency forges strange alliances*, he thought. *Pettigrew is doubtless writhing in his watery grave at the thought of the Avenger run by pirates, but in my place, what would he have done differently?* Finding no answer, he put his shoulder to the gun they were sighting and helped Diego's men roll it into place.

Diego sighted along the twenty-four pounder's barrel. He and his men had trained the Avenger's guns to fire into an area twenty-feet square. Instead of raking the Votrelec as would be common practice, Diego hoped with a single desperate volley to blast a hole through the ship's hull and sink her to the bottom of the harbor and Varlek's coffin with it. Separated from his refuge, the vampire might become vulnerable and give them a chance to destroy him.

Above on deck, others were lashing every firearm to the railing.

Without silver balls, the muskets may not be effective against the red eyes or the white eyes, but whatever humans stood on deck were worthy targets.

Once the muskets were in place, the grisly work of propping the corpses of the Avenger's crew beside them began. Pike lifted the torso of a Marine torn in two at the waist to set him on a barrel, and his innards fell to the deck with a greasy splatter. "Hell can't be any worse," he said.

Beside him, Abelard laughed bitterly. "If this scheme doesn't work, we'll find out soon enough."

"Even if it does."

When they finished, Diego and Brackenridge surveyed their handiwork. Bodies climbed the rigging, stood at the capstans, slouched in the prow. Gore stained uniforms, empty eye sockets, and missing limbs. "There's a crew fit to frighten the Devil himself," said Diego.

"They'd have frightened him enough when they were alive," Brackenridge replied. "They scared you didn't they?"

"I'm not the Devil. Their number and their guns gave me pause, I'll admit, but frightened? Never."

"The more fool you."

"Perhaps so, but it doesn't matter now."

Brackenridge nodded agreement. "True enough. But when this is over—"

"When this is over?" Diego laughed. "When this is over, we can resume our differences, if we both still live. For now, we have an enemy in common."

The guns were loaded and primed, the fuses were set, and now all the men on the Avenger could do was wait for the sun to sink into the sea.

LXXXV

The sun set. Varlek and the Anointed rose. The Votrelec lay at anchor in Armonia's harbor as the *trúdovi* were brought aboard. Soon, the ship would sail for Cuerpo Santo, and deliver terror to the island and its people.

"Can you bring the Votrelec close enough into the harbor to fire the cannon at the church?" Varlek asked Sergi.

The Russian rubbed his chin. He feared disappointing Varlek again in the same day but had to be truthful. "I am sorry, Master; it is too shallow

"Hell can't be any worse."

close to shore. I have no charts of the harbor. There may be reefs and sandbars I don't know about. We could founder. The tide is high now, and I might be able to sail in closer to shore, but I can't be sure the guns would reach the church."

"I need only one volley. I want to knock that cursed icon from the roof, and break up that abatis, if I can. I want you to sail in as close as you can, fire a volley, and sail out again."

"If you hit the church, you may kill a number of people inside – destroy potential subjects," Batteaux said.

Varlek pondered this for a moment. "Perhaps you are right. We'll let the *trúdovi* do their part, and once the cross is down, the Anointed can attack the defenders, who will never withstand the assault."

Varlek knew that his vampires could not enter the church, but the *trúdovi* could, and they would drive the islanders from their sanctuary. Once they no longer had the church's protection, they would be his.

He was especially looking forward to killing the priest, the priest who was a stone in his boot, the priest who knew too much, the priest who gathered the islanders into his church like a hen gathers her brood. He had dealt with holy men before many times and had never lost. What his Anointed could not do, the *trúdovi* could, and what the *trúdovi* could not do, the small cadre of humans who served him could.

Varlek wanted the priest taken alive and brought to him stripped of his vestments, his icons, and holy water, just a man, and Varlek would teach him his place. He would make the priest kneel and beg, renounce his faith, worship him.

Perhaps he would turn the priest into one of the Anointed, just as he had turned Sebastian's friend into one of the *trúdovi*. He smiled in amusement at the thought. Or perhaps he would simply flay him alive like the Church's revered Saint Bartholomew, peel his skin from him in long painful strips then throw him raw and bleeding into the sea for the sharks.

Or perhaps he would let the priest live, keep him in a cage and let him sorrow at what his flock had become, worshippers of a demon. That might be the most cruel of torments.

Vapors rose from the water along with a scant quarter moon. Varlek smiled. Their approach would be masked. They would slip into Cuerpo Santo's harbor and suddenly burst from the curtain of mist into full view as if by magic, he standing on the bowsprit over the figurehead of the full-bosomed woman with a Death's-head for a face, a headsman's axe clutched in her hands. It was an image that few who saw lived to remember. In another life, he had been a performer in a traveling show, and he understood the value of a grand entrance.

"It is time." Varlek said to Batteaux and Sergi. "Weigh anchor."

LXXXVI

Diego and his men spent hours before sunset muffling anything on the Avenger that would clank, creak, or rattle. He wanted nothing to betray their advance on the Votrelec. Luck was with them. The mist was rising and they should be able to approach Cuerpo Santo unseen. Now they would also approach unheard.

The pirates scampered up and down the rigging and across the spars like squirrels in an oak tree, preparing the two foresails that they hoped would ease the Avenger forward. They could not predict the timing

"What do you think, Brio?"

The helmsman turned his face into the gentle wind that pushed the ship from the North. "We haven't much wind, Diego, but we haven't far to sail, either. I just hope it doesn't chase the fog away."

"I'm not worried. You could sail a ship into the Devil's pocket," Pike said with a laugh.

"*Si*," said Brio. "And tonight I may be doing just that."

Brackenridge came on deck with his hand-carved weapon in his grip. "If we corner him, let me be the one to kill Varlek. Promise me that."

"What can a man promise of the heat of battle? Who knows what may happen? Let me promise you this: if it comes down to you killing Varlek, or me killing him, I promise you I will step aside."

Brackenridge's chin dipped in a nod of acceptance, and he walked to the rail, where he stood, staring over the water, his thumb stroking the tip of his stake as if he were burnishing it to a high sheen.

"He's mad," Pike said under his breath.

Diego looked across the deck at the dead men arrayed behind the muskets. "As are we all, Pike, as are we all."

"Well, my Johnny Bull ancestors have a saying: Fate often saves a man if courage be good."

"My ancestors have a saying too," said Brio grimly: "Those whom the gods wish to destroy, they first make mad."

LXXXVIII

In the church, patience had frayed to the breaking point. Quarrels broke out. Despite rationing, the water was all but gone. Children cried and their mothers wept while outside, the men strained weary eyes for any sight of a coming attack.

"I wish they'd just come at us and get it over with," Bela, one of the islanders said.

"That's part of their game," Vargas said, eyes fixed on the clearing. "Making us think. When you're fighting, you don't think much, perhaps not at all. No time to doubt yourself or your plans. Sitting idle, that's when you start to wonder, and your imagination takes over. You start asking yourself, 'Did I set the flint properly on my musket? Is my dagger sharp enough?' when you already know that you did all the right things to prepare for a fight. Then you start making your enemy bigger, more skillful, more powerful than he really is, and you imagine confronting him and losing the fight. That's what the vampire wants."

Vargas looked into a distance beyond the trees. "Once we fought a French privateer, the LeMarque. They paced us for three days when they could have easily overtaken us, tiring us and letting us stew about the coming fight. When the LeMarque finally attacked, an exploding shell killed a crewman named Vasco, a young man on his first voyage with the Hand. The LeMarque's crew boarded us, but we repelled them.

"After the battle, I picked up Vasco's musket from the deck. The ramrod was halfway into the barrel. He was loading it when the shelling began. When I pushed the rod, it would go no further. He had loaded it six or seven times in his nervousness. Had he fired it, it would have blown up in his face. That is why the vampire waits. Unlike a sword or dagger, a man holds his edge only so long."

"How do you prevent it?"

"I do two things." He held up his musket and pointed to a thread dangling from the trigger guard. "I ready my musket and I tie the thread to remind me that I did. That way, I don't have to think about it."

"And the other?"

Vargas grinned. "I think instead of bedding a woman, imagine every detail of her body, the texture of her hair above and below, the soft curves of her flesh and the hard curves of her hip bones, the strength of her hands and her thighs as she locks her legs around my middle, and her panting breath in my ear."

He looked up and saw Father Beppo staring at him. "My son," he said to Vargas, "would you be shrived before the battle? When was your last confession?"

"Many years, Father," Vargas replied. "Perhaps after the battle, if we are both standing, I'll take your offer, but not now. Sometimes it takes a sinner to fight the Devil, eh? Less to lose."

Beppo said, "At least allow me this." He poured a few drops of water from the flask on his fingertips and leaned forward to touch Vargas's forehead, making a clean cross on the pirate's soot-stained face.

Vargas looked away, embarrassed. "I apologize, Father. A pirate's life makes one cynical, I fear."

"My son, there is always hope, and there is always redemption. When this fight is over, I will receive you gladly, and so will the Savior."

Beppo would have given communion to everyone, but any wine in the church was used to cleanse the wounds and ease the pain of the injured and dying; nor was there flour to bake the wafers. He did what he saw as the best alternative, and with his flask of holy water, drew the sign of the cross on the foreheads of every one of the flock. If it would not protect them in the battle to come, it would at least provide them some solace in their last moments.

LXXXIX

Cataldo's sentries hid in the trees, watching the harbor. The mist had risen earlier, obscuring the entrance, and the light from the silver paring of the moon was little help.

"Do you hear something?" one said to the other.

"No. Wait – creaking."

"Yes. Out on the water."

They peered into the gloom and saw nothing then saw everything. Dozens of torches flared to light on the Votrelec, and the glowing ship glided from the mist into the harbor.

The watchmen ran to the church to sound the alarm.

Longboats were lowered, with the *trúdovi* on board, each boat accompanied by one of Varlek's human henchmen. The white-eyes pulled mindlessly at the oars until they reached the shore, then climbed from the boats with their stabbing, slashing, and smashing weapons clutched in their bony fingers. They grouped on the beach and stood, silent, awaiting their orders.

The anointed followed in boats of their own; their eyes glowing, hungry for the fight, and hungry for the blood of the islanders in the church. When his force was assembled on the shore, Varlek was the last, in a boat with Batteaux. He left Sergi in charge of the ship with a handful of the crew, men and *trúdovi*, and stepped onto the island to lead his force to the fight.

Batteaux asked Varlek if he were going to bring the children ashore to parade them in front of the church as leverage. The vampire simply shook his head and said, "It would not make a difference. The children are not theirs." When he followed Varlek to the church, Batteaux noticed the vampire didn't come as close to the abatis as he had the night before. Perhaps he's learned some caution, thought Batteaux. These islanders are no fools.

Varlek stood tall, naked under a cloak that he spread with his arms like great red wings, his unnatural manhood on arrogant display. "People of the Exiles," his voice was a low velvet rasp but heard by everyone inside the barricade. He waited a moment, and when no response came, he called out again.

"In the name of the Savior, I command you, get thee behind me Satan!" Father Beppo had climbed over the barricade before the men could stop him. He held the church's crucifix high in front of him. It seemed to glow on its own in the priest's hands.

Varlek hissed and averted his eyes. He spoke without looking to a tall, cadaverous man with a long chin, a high domed head, and long arms that put his hands at his knees, who stood behind him. "Rodescu! *Támadás!*" The tall man snarled a guttural command in the language of the *trúdovi* and waved his arms like a musical conductor or a puppeteer, and a pack of them burst from the clearing behind Varlek. They passed the vampire and began scuttling across the packed earth of the courtyard toward Beppo.

When they were halfway to the barricade, Vargas gave a signal, and two cannons were touched off at once, each firing a ball linked to the other by a chain. The links whistled through the air, and the chain cut the advancing *trúdovi* in two. Their legs lay twitching on the ground and their torsos flailed at the earth as they tried to crawl to their intended victim.

Cataldo vaulted over the abatis and grabbed Beppo around the waist.

"No," the priest said. "I will stand and fight."

"You're no good to us dead," Cataldo snarled, and heaved Beppo back inside the barricade. He looked over his shoulder and saw a white-eyed horde shambling across the courtyard. He climbed onto the abatis and his shirt caught on one of the sharpened stakes. It took only seconds to tear himself loose, but by then, bony hands had hold of his legs, dragging him from the tangled limbs.

Taloned fingers dug into Cataldo's shoulder and he brought down his fist like a hammer on the arm, snapping bone, and the fingers lost their grip. He grabbed the hammer from the creature and swung it into its face. He struck a second one, its fingers dug into his leg as it tried to climb his body to get at his throat. A third loomed at him and he swung the hammer around to cram the handle into its mouth and hold it at bay while he found his footing.

He was nearly over the top when another *trúdovi* wrapped its arms around his legs and tried to pull him back. Strong hands reached over the barricade and grabbed his shoulders. Mobuti dragged Cataldo over, and the *trúdovi* with him. The African locked the creature's head between his huge hands and squeezed until it burst, spraying his face and chest with foul ichor.

Behind him, two of the invaders had a screaming islander in their grip and were clawing chunks of flesh from his body. Another had his teeth in the throat of one of the pirates who fought vainly to pry the jaws loose.

Dozens of *trúdovi* stormed the abatis, but they found climbing one-handed over the tangled stakes awkward, holding onto their weapons. This made them easier prey for the defenders.

One of the *trúdovi* landed in the courtyard, a boathook in its hands. Vargas swung his cutlass in a wide arc from below his hip. It struck the *trúdovi's* neck, and its head flopped to the side, held by a stalk of stringy gristle. The creature fell backward, its rags catching on the branches and holding its grotesque body upright as if it were still in the battle.

"The water! The water!" Cataldo shouted. From either side of the church, men tipped the casks of sanctified water, pouring them into the shallow moat around the church. *Trúdovi* scrambled over the abatis, driving the defenders back. The monsters splashed through the holy moat without incident.

Cataldo and the men with him fought the monsters back from the church doors, but gunfire and screams from the churchyard told him that they were being attacked from all sides.

They move as one, Vargas thought. They don't think for themselves. He looked across the courtyard and saw a man standing beside Varlek. He was taller than the vampire, and lean, with long arms. He was waving those arms now, moving them like a conductor. Vargas took careful aim and fired his musket. The tall man's head exploded in a spray of blood and brains. His body fell backward, and as it did, the *trúdovi* froze.

"Quickly!" Vargas shouted. "Their heads. Smash their heads." He picked up a fired musket and swung it two-handed over his shoulder like an axe at a *trúdovi's* head, and felt the skull cave in. Others followed suit, and by the time Varlek had control of the *trúdovi*, few of them were still moving inside the barricade.

Varlek seethed. He turned to Batteaux. "It is time to loose the Anointed."

LXXXIX

Brackenridge stood by the helm of the Avenger. His ship, but his ship no more. He hated the deal with the Devil he'd had to strike, letting the mongrel buccaneers take command, but how else could he avenge his crew on the monster Varlek?

The Avenger glided toward Cuerpo Santo's harbor. The torches on the Votrelec were visible through the mist for almost a league, and with what wind the foresails could catch, Brio angled the ship toward the blaze of light.

"The torches are all on the land side," Pike said. "That'll help conceal our approach."

"And they'll be watching the shore unless I miss my guess." Diego turned to Brio. "It's all up to you now, my friend."

"*Si*," Brio said. "And luck."

The breeze stiffened and the Avenger crept forward. Diego wished he could have brought the Belladonna to the fight, with his own ship and crew, he could face anyone or anything, but Fate put him at this time and in this place, and he had no choice but to make one last roll of the dice.

"Remember your promise, lo Mano," Brackenridge said, clutching his stake.

"I haven't forgotten it."

"Killing Varlek won't bring my crew back from the dead," the Englishman said, "but it will give their souls some peace."

XC

S ergi stood on the deck of the Votrelec listening to the crack of the rifles and the screams of the islanders from the church. Most of the *trúdovi* were ashore, as were all of Varlek's Anointed. The Russian was surprised that the islanders had resisted Varlek at all, let alone fought his minions a second time. He had let the invaders ashore then sailed back to the harbor's entrance so as to not be trapped by shallows when the tide went out. The Votrelec lay at anchor now, and Sergi was hopeful that tonight's victory would please Varlek enough to set aside his earlier failures.

A cry from behind made him turn. "Sergi! A ship."

He stared dumbstruck at the sight of the Avenger drifting silently from the mist not five fathoms from his starboard bow. He would have ordered the starboard gun ports open, but there weren't enough crew to fire them. They were ashore attacking the church.

XCI

T he Anointed dashed like shadows across the courtyard, leaping over the abatis as if it were a garden fence, landing inside and viciously attacking the defenders. They fell upon the men, ravenous for blood.

Varlek stood across the courtyard, waiting in the safety of the trees. The defenders knew enough to fire silver from their muskets, and he couldn't chance being hit. The humans may have resisted the *trúdovi*, but they were no match for the fury of the Anointed. When he thought the islanders were sufficiently subdued, he would call off the attack. He didn't want them all dead. He wanted them demoralized and compliant.

One of the islanders dropped his musket and turned to run in panic. He got two steps before one of the red eyed monsters leapt on his back and brought him down, ripping open his throat and gorging itself. Mobuti grabbed the vampire by the shoulders and slammed him onto the abatis, impaling him on one of the sharpened limbs. The vampire howled and writhed for a moment, then the light went out of its crimson eyes, and it was still.

Raoul fell backwards as a vampire pounced on him. He had his forearm across its throat, holding its fangs away from his neck. The creature snarled, snapping its jaws. Raoul pulled a crucifix from his pocket, and instead of showing it to the vampire, he shoved it into its eye where the icon smoked and smoldered.

The vampire rolled off Raoul and into the moat. As soon as its body touched the holy water, it burst into a searing blue flame.

The vampires could be killed, but it was obvious to Cataldo that the defenders were losing the fight. The islanders were no match for Varlek's minions. When he saw the effect the holy water had on the vampire, he shouted, "Back! Inside the moat."

One of the vampires seized Vasco by his shoulders and sank his fangs into the pirate's shoulder. Vasco fired his pistol, sending a silver ball into its body. The vampire screeched and fell back, smoke coming from a hole in its chest. It let go of Vasco and clawed at its flesh, trying to dig the ball out. It screeched again when its fingers closed on the silver and drew them out, smoking. Vasco picked up a fallen musket, praying it was loaded with silver, and shot the vampire through the heart.

Father Beppo came out of the church holding the carved crucifix from behind the altar as if were a sledge. He waded into a pack of vampires savaging one of his flock, bludgeoning the killers with it, shouting in Latin. He struck the first of them across the back of the head, and the edge of the wood broke through the back of the creature's skull. Its head turned toward this new attacker, and Beppo swung the cross to strike it full in the fore head. The vampire's skull split, and it fell away, howling and clawing at the wound.

From the distance, a roar made everyone pause, if only for an instant. Cannon fire from the harbor followed by the rattle of muskets. Varlek's head whipped around. "What is happening?" he snapped to Batteaux. "Find out." Suddenly, triumph gave way to doubt. Batteaux set off at a run for the harbor. Was the Votrelec under attack?

Both had the same thought: Francine.

XCII

Diego watched over the barrel of the center gun as the Avenger came alongside the Votrelec. When he was certain the volley would strike the Votrelec amidships, he struck flint to steel and lit the fuse that branched outward like fingers of sputtering fire to the entire battery of guns. He had timed the fuses well. Nearly all twenty-two guns roared within a few seconds, shelling the Votrelec with a deadly volley. The barbed fire shot raked the sails and rigging, catching them afire. Diego could see movement on deck as the Votrelec's crew tried to douse the flames.

"Muskets!" Diego shouted, and his men ran from corpse to corpse, pulling triggers and raking the deck with musket fire.

One of the balls hit Sergi in the chest, and he staggered backward, holding onto the main mast for support. Air sucked through the hole with a bubbling gurgle. Georg, one of his human crewmen, came running. "Sergi! The hull is breached. We're taking on water."

The Russian tried to give an order, but breath failed him, and he slumped to the deck to die.

The Avenger drifted closer, and Diego's men could choose their targets. The torches on the island side of the Votrelec made sharp targets of the silhouettes on her deck. They aimed for the heads of the *trúdovi*, killing them once and for all when they found their mark. The white eyes shambled aimlessly around the deck. The person who had commanded them was dead, leaving them for the moment under no control.

"We have to board the Votrelec before she sinks," Brackenridge said. "We have to rescue the children."

"There are only a handful of us. We don't know how many of those things are on board," Diego said.

"We have to try. They'll drown if they're locked up on board."

"All right," Diego said. "Reload some of the muskets and lower a boat."

Diego left Brio and two others on the Avenger and with Brackenridge, rowed across the gap between the vessels, towing two long boats behind them at Brackenridge's insistence, in the event they found the children. In his arrogant confidence, Varlek had made no provision for defending the Votrelec, and they met no resistance approaching the ship.

As they rowed toward the Votrelec, they saw the ragged hole the barrage had blown in the ship's hull. "We can climb in through there," said Pike, pointing at the opening.

"That's a good idea," Diego said. "Who knows what we might meet climbing up the anchor chain." The water was waist deep in the hold and rising. "Brackenridge, you go with Santiago to look for the children."

"What are you going to do?"

"Find Varlek's coffin and destroy it."

Corpses floated in the murky water in the hold, some of them human, some not, but the pirates found none moving. "This way." Diego led them to rough wooden steps that climbed to the main deck.

Above was a scene from the Devil's nightmares. In the glow of the flaming sails, the *trúdovi* hunched over dead crewmen, gorging themselves on their still warm flesh, tearing gobbets from the corpses and stuffing them into their maws. Pike aimed at the head of one of them and Diego stayed his hand. "Let them alone," he whispered hoarsely."If they're busy eating their own, they won't notice us."

He was regrettably mistaken. One of the *trúdovi* looked up from his grisly meal and saw the pirates. He smelled fresher meat and rose from his crouch, his maw of broken teeth gaping. He snarled and charged them, claws reaching for their throats. Diego swung his cutlass overhand and clove the creature's skull to its nose.

The pirates ran for the passageway that led to the Captain's cabin. The *trúdovi* tried to follow, but Diego shot the first one in the corridor through his head. A second fell over the body and was dispatched by Pike with a blow from a sledge. The fallen *trúdovi* blocked the passageway and Diego and the others were able to reach the doors to the cabin before the white-eyes could follow.

The main cabin was dimly lit by gimbaled lanterns. The men piled furniture against the door to keep the *trúdovi* out and then they turned to the oversized ebony coffin that lay across wooden trestles. Diego tried to raise the lid, but it wouldn't move.

"Locked. Give me your sledge."

Pike handed him the hammer and Diego splintered the wood around the latch. He heaved again, and the lid swung upward.

They gasped to see a beautiful young woman sleeping inside it.

"She's one them – his mistress," said Pike "Kill her."

"No, wait," said Diego. He took the crucifix from his pocket and laid it on the sleeping girl's breast. Instead of recoiling in pain, the young woman sighed and her eyes blinked open. Her eyes wandered from face to face, still half dazed.

"She's human," one of the others said.

"Yes, but she's in some kind of trance. We're taking her with us."

"Are you mad?"

"If she's special to Varlek, we can use her to bargain."

There was a crash followed by others. The *trúdovi* were breaking down the cabin door.

Diego pulled aside a thick curtain from the stern windows. "We can't hope to win against those monsters." He picked up a chair and smashed out the glass and frame. "We'll have to jump and take our chances. I hope those things are poor swimmers."

One by one, the pirates climbed through the window casement and dropped to the water below. Diego was last, and lowered Francine as far as he could by her arms to Pike, who began swimming around the side of the Votrelec to their longboat, his arm across her chest.

Diego took a lamp from its mounting and threw it into the coffin, breaking the glass. The oil caught and soon the lining was burning with a dark acrid smoke. The cabin door began to splinter. Diego pulled the curtain closed over the broken window before he climbed through the casement. If they can't think for themselves, he reasoned, maybe they can't think at all.

XCIII

In the forward part of the hold, Brackenridge and Santiago followed the screams and cries of the children. They waded through the compartment filled with floating coffins and found the Votrelec's brig. All three cells held children. Brackenridge recognized some of them as those he had rescued then had taken from the Avenger.

He took a lantern from its peg and searched the walls, looking for a key to open the cells, but there was no key to be found. "Damn it," he said. "There's no key, and no guard here to search for one. He must have gone on deck when the attack began."

Santiago said. "Stand aside, Captain. I haven't sailed with the Hand for so many years without learning a few skills. He drew a long stiletto from his boot and slipped it into the keyhole of the first cell. He probed the lock for a moment, and with a twist of the blade threw back the deadbolt. In a moment, all three cells were open and the children were free.

"Follow us," Santiago said to the children, "We're taking you away from here."

They led the children through the hold to the hole in the hull, which seemed much smaller now because the Votrelec was sinking. "Quickly," Santiago said, "through here."

He helped the children through the hole in the hull, and Brackenridge, standing in the longboat, lifted them in. When that boat was filled, he stepped to a second boat. Brackenridge heard splashing, and turned to see shapes swimming toward him. He drew his pistol.

"Don't shoot." Diego's voice.

Santiago was putting the last few children through the hole when one of them screamed. One of the *trúdovi* had seized a little girl and was about to sink his teeth into her. Santiago clubbed the white-eyes with a doubled fist, knocking him backward, but it hung onto the child, dragging her underwater with it.

The *trúdovi* suddenly reared up out of the water and attacked the bigger target. Its hands gripped Santiago's arms and its fingers dug into his flesh. Santiago head butted the creature, which loosened its grip for a few seconds, long enough for the pirate to drive his dagger through one of the egg-white eyes. He twisted the blade, and the creature slumped under the water.

The girl was sobbing and choking on swallowed water. Santiago grabbed her and pushed her through the hole. "She is the last," he shouted to Brackenridge. I –"

Another of the *trúdovi* came boiling from the water and clamped its jaws on Santiago's neck. It pulled him under, and he didn't come back.

Brackenridge cut the rope holding the long boat and pushed off to get far away from the Votrelec as quickly as possible.

They were bringing the children aboard the Avenger when the fire reached the Votrelec's powder magazine and it went up with a roar, breaking the ship nearly in two.

XCIV

A t the church, the defenders retreated inside the moat of holy water. The first of the vampires who splashed into it shrieked as the moat became a ring of blue fire that climbed his legs to his torso. The other vampires hung back, unsure what to do.

Varlek was furious. What should have been a rout was turning into an expensive loss.

Batteaux came running, out of breath. "Varlek," he panted, "The Votrelec is on fire and she is sinking."

"The coffins. The Anointed will have no refuge." The vampire's mind raced. "Come with me." They ran, Varlek quickly leaving Batteaux panting behind him unable to match the vampire's speed.

Varlek knew that without their coffins, many of his vampires would fall victim to the sunlight or be helpless hiding from the sun in whatever dark place they could find. His forces dwindling, he could not hope to take the islands and enslave their people. As he and Batteaux rounded the last bend in the road to the harbor, Varlek saw the Votrlec in flames, sinking into the water, and behind it, the Avenger.

"Get me to the ship," Varlek hissed.

Batteaux untied a skiff from the mooring and he and Varlek climbed aboard. Batteaux rowed while Varlek stood in the bow, his eyes blazing and his face a twisted mask of fury. His plan was falling apart, his wish for a kingdom to go unfulfilled.

If nothing else, he would return to Cuerpo Santo and kill the priest, whom he saw as the root of his trouble. Then he would launch a new wave of terror every night, killing man, woman, and child, and building a new cadre of Anointed, and *trúdovi*. This battle may be lost, but he would triumph in the end. The Votrelec was low in the water when Varlek and Batteaux climbed aboard. The sails were burned to charred rags and the fire had spread to the forecastle, which blazed and crackled. The deck was splintered by the powder explosion, and Varlek saw bodies of *trúdovi* and humans alike, sprawled across its length. A few *trúdovi* wandered aimlessly around the deck.

Varlek stepped to the passageway that led to his cabin and saw the splintered door and beyond it, the flames. The vampire roared in rage and smashed his fist through the bulkhead. He had changed his mind. He would kill them all. Behind him, Batteaux's heart sank. "No, no, no," he sobbed, falling to his knees.

The vampire pulled him roughly to his feet. "Take me to that ship."

XCV

Brackenridge and Diego put the children in the hold where they would be out of danger and returned to the helm where Pike was staring at the Votrelec through a spyglass. "On the deck, Diego. I see two people moving."

Diego peered through the glass and saw the red eyes of the vampire staring back at him. He felt the vampire reaching into his mind and dropped the telescope, shaking his head. "Varlek."

"Now would be a good time to sail away," said Pike.

"If I had a full crew, I would."

Brackenridge pointed to the Votrelec. "They're lowering a boat." He stared in disbelief. "They're rowing toward us."

Diego could see Varlek, Batteaux, and a half dozen *trúdovi* at the oars. "Can we ready a gun? Blow them out of the water?"

"Sure enough," said Pike, "but by the time we do, they'll be too close for aim."

"We can't abandon ship and leave the children to that monster. We have to stand and fight."

Brackenridge's grip tightened on his pointed stake. "Then let them come."

XCVI

Inside the church, the islanders cowered at the fearful sounds from the outside. The vampires stood beyond the blue fire of the moat, howling in frustration, lusting for the blood they smelled inside. A few *trúdovi* wandered aimlessly, snarling and tearing at the corpses that lay just inside the abatis.

Father Beppo stood at the church entrance like a sentry, holding the crucifix in front of him with both hands. Every time one of the Anointed looked toward the church doors, its head quickly twitched away.

One of Diego's men, seeing the effect the water in the moat had on the vampires, ran to it, scooped a double handful and threw it into the face of one of the monsters. The creature's skin smoked and sizzled. The pirate crouched for more of the holy water, and another vampire swooped

"Take me to that ship!"

in, seizing the pirate's head between its hands and yanked him across the moat to be pounced upon by its fellows.

Cataldo stared in horror as the vampires sank their fangs into their victim's flesh. "We are at a stalemate, *Padre*," Cataldo said, clenching and unclenching his fists. "They cannot come in, and we cannot leave. They will starve us out, or we will die of thirst."

"It is only a few hours until sunrise. The vampires will have to retreat or die. They –"

Beppo's words were cut off by a loud crash. Behind the church, the *trúdovi* had cut down a tall palm tree that fell across the churchyard and landed against the back wall of the church, spanning the distance between the barricade and the roof. A quick-thinking islander threw a lamp at the tree trunk. The lamp shattered, and the burning oil soon had the tree in flames. Two of the *trúdovi* were set aflame, and others hung back, so that only a few made it to the church roof.

They scampered over the top of the tree, this time to break through the thatching, plunge through the roof, and land below amid the screaming flock.

Cataldo rushed into the nave and saw a fallen monster, a leg broken in the fall, whirling on its good leg and clawing at anyone within reach. Cataldo pushed through the throng of panicked people, as they rushed back from peril. He lifted the injured *trúdovi* over his head, and brought it down across the altar with a wet crunch like the breaking of a rotting tree limb. The creature snarled and flopped on the floorboards like a landed fish. Cataldo raised one of the heavy candlesticks from the altar and clubbed the *trúdovi* with it again and again until it stopped moving.

A second of the white-eyed demons dropped through the roof to land on Cataldo's back, knocking him to the floor. The creature sank its fangs into his shoulder and wrapped its bony arms around his neck.

The people in the church stared in shock and horror as the monster tore at Cataldo's flesh. One old man, stooped and picked up the fallen candlestick and swung it over his head with both hands, hammering the *trúdovi's* skull. Galvanized by his action, others joined him, screaming this time, in rage instead of terror, picking up whatever they could find and beating the monster until it no longer had a whole bone.

Father Beppo rushed in to the fallen Cataldo and poured water from his flask into the raw wound where the *trúdovi* had gnawed a gory crescent from his skin and muscle. The holy water bubbled and steamed for a moment then was still.

"Bind his wounds," Beppo told one of the women and ran back to the entrance.

XCVII

The longboat bumped against the hull of the Avenger. On deck, Brackenridge, Diego and his handful of men stood ready. As the first *trúdovi* showed its head over the taffrail, Pike blew it off with a blunderbuss. A second and a third crawled over. Muskets blazed, but missed their mark. The *trúdovi* came at the pirates, claws raised and growling.

Swords were drawn, and as the white-eyes charged, Diego's men found them difficult adversaries. More *trúdovi* came aboard. Diego counted six in the boat, and these seemed to be the last. He shot one through the forehead with his pistol and was drawing his cutlass when he heard a voice behind him.

"Foolish."

Diego whirled to see Varlek and Batteaux standing by the starboard rail. They had used the *trúdovi* as a diversion while they came aboard.

"You!" Varlek pointed a long finger at Brackenridge. "You dare to still challenge me?"

The scene went suddenly quiet as Diego's man dispatched the last of the *trúdovi*. All that could be heard was the ragged panting of the defenders' breath.

"I see you have made clever use of your dead. So shall I."

Varklek raised his hands and began chanting an incantation. From the corner of his eye, Diego saw the corpses of the English sailors and Marines begin to twitch and move. One of them turned its ruined face toward him and its white eyes blinked open.

Varlek continued his chanting and Diego realized that he had to stop him before the vampire turned the whole dead crew into his henchmen. He drew the silver crucifix dagger from his belt and charged the vampire, interrupting his incantation.

He slashed at the protective forearm the vampire threw up, the silver edge opening a long wound from his wrist nearly to his elbow. Varlek shrieked in surprise and pain. He had no time to look at the smoking gash because Diego was parrying to thrust the blade into his body. Varlek swung his uninjured arm across his chest and struck Diego alongside his jaw, lifting him from the deck and knocking him a good ten feet into a pile of rope. The silver dagger skittered across the deck to the toe of Batteaux's boot.

Brackenridge roared in anger and rushed at the vampire, his stake braced against his hip like a lance. Varlek sidestepped the thrust and delivered a blow that sent the Englishman sprawling. His stake went spinning through the open hatch into the hold.

Varlek leapt across the deck and landed with his knees in the Englishman's stomach and his hands around Brackenridge's throat. He leered in triumph. "Batteaux! Order my new minions to kill these men." His fingers tightened around Brackenridge's throat and try as he might, the Englishman could not pry those taloned fingers from his windpipe. "You destroyed my ship, so I'll take yours and your dead crew to sail her."

Hearing no command from Batteaux, Varlek shouted, "Batteaux, did you not hear me? Give the order."

Batteaux looked back to the burning ship then to the crucifix dagger lying at his feet. He picked it up and said one word: "Francine."

He ran at his master, and before Varlek could turn or move away, Batteaux plunged the silver dagger through Varlek's back and out his chest. The vampire howled in agony as blue fire blossomed around the edges of the wound. He tried desperately to reach his hands over his shoulders to pluck out the weapon. One hand closed on the crucifix handle, and flames burst through his fingers, making him let go.

Varlek's eyes widened and he rose to his feet, whirling like a dog chasing its tail. When he faced the mast, Diego rushed at him, clutched the crucifix with both hands, and slammed the vampire into the mast, driving the point into the wood. He scooped a belaying pin from the deck and used it to pound the dagger deeper into the oak.

Varlek's talons dug parallel furrows in the mast as he tried to get a grip that would help him. He wailed in pain and writhed like an insect on a pin, hands reaching vainly to pull the silver blade from his back.

Before their fascinated eyes, Varlek began to wilt like an emptying wineskin, the smooth skin wrinkling as his body sagged into itself. As his face shrank, his eyes bulged like onyx eggs with jagged forks of lightning dancing across their surface. He arms fell helpless to his sides, and the vampire's flesh quickly turned to sand that poured through his bones and formed a grey mound at his skeletal feet.

The resurrected crewmen stood immobile, waiting for a command.

All eyes turned to Batteaux. Diego picked up a cutlass from the deck and said, "Are you going to kill us all now? Avenge your master? If so, then do it quickly."

Batteaux opened his mouth to speak but before he could, a voice called out, "Father?" He turned to see Francine standing across the deck between two of the white-eyed crewmen. He spoke a command in the *trúdovi* language, and moving with a unity not unlike a school of fish, the white-eyed crew turned and stepped, staggered, or dragged themselves to the port rail where they climbed over and threw themselves like lemmings into the sea.

Pike raised a pistol and pointed it at Batteaux's head. "Before he changes his mind."

"Hold," Diego said.

Francine went to her father, her steps unsure. He held out his arms to her and they embraced.

"I don't think he's a threat any longer. Put down your weapon, but don't put it away."

In the east, the sky was lightening. Soon it would be dawn.

XCVIII

At the church, the Anointed suddenly stopped their attack. They stood still and turned their heads, listening, sniffing at the air. Something had happened that the vampires sensed but the humans could not. Some began a keening wail and beat at their heads with their fists. Others raged, and began wrenching limbs from the abatis and hurling them at the church, knocking defenders off their feet. Then, as if a collective decision had been made, the vampires climbed over the barricade and ran into the trees, leaving the *trúdovi* behind.

"They're heading for the ship," Cataldo said.

"The sun will rise soon," Father Beppo said, looking up at the false dawn. "They must return to their coffins."

Vargas peered over the abatis. "That leaves only the white-eyes to fight. Our odds are improving."

"More than you may think," said Cataldo. "Before, they acted as one mind. Now, they seem to act at random. It may be time for us to go on the attack. He picked up a sledge and shouted, "With me, then," and climbed over the barrier.

The remaining *trúdovi* saw the men coming and the fight was quick and vicious. The *trúdovi* clawed and bit, and the defenders clubbed and slashed. Limbs were hacked off, leaving *trúdovi* crawling in the dirt and clawing at the legs of their enemies. Cataldo and his men smashed their skulls with hammers, clubs, and rifle butts. In moments, it was done. No *trúdovi* were left moving in the courtyard.

Cataldo wiped the dark foul gore from his face. Beppo came up behind him. "At sunrise, we go to the Votrelec, open their coffins, and destroy them all."

XCIX

On the Avenger, Diego watched the dock through his spyglass. The first coral wash of dawn tinged the eastern sky as the vampires returned. Finding the ship in flames, they beat at their faces with their fists and capered in rage. Some of them ran to the trees in search of shelter from the coming sunrise. Others plunged into the surf and began swimming desperately for their ship to coffins that were destroyed either by the explosion or the fire.

"What do we do, Diego?" said Brio. "Some of them may survive."

"Perhaps." He lowered the glass. "But we know them now and their weaknesses. Their numbers are lessened, and they have lost their master, so they have no direction."

That is true," said Batteaux from behind them. "They were simple thralls to Varlek. They no longer have wills of their own."

Diego nodded. "Some may survive, but the islanders will hunt them down. The people of the Exiles are no longer easy prey, if ever they were."

The first rays of the sun cut through the morning mist. The vampires on the Votrelec were all below in the hold by this time, but the pirates saw figures moving on the deck. Diego peered through the telescope. "They are not white-eyed, nor vampires. They are men." The pair were dragging a fallen sail to cover the open hatch and block the sun.

He handed the glass to Batteaux," who put it to his eye. "Krilencu and Vochs, two of Varlek's daylight henchmen. Human rats. Sadistic torturers." Batteaux spat. "Varlek chose them because they enjoy their work." He walked away to the prow where Francine sat, staring across the water.

The men looked toward Diego and he nodded. Brio and Pike raised muskets and took aim. They fired almost as one, and the pair on the Votrelec fell.

"I wouldn't try to board her until the fires are out," Diego said, "but before the sun sets, we will search her end to end and kill every one of them that we find, vampire or man. Brackenridge, may get to use his stake yet." He looked across the deck where Brackenridge sat with a lap desk across his knees. He was recording the names of his dead crew in the Avenger's log.

"Why don't he just write 'all hands lost' and be done with it?" Pike said.

"Every man deals with grief in his own way. To be handed a command and all be lost in a day, I don't know what I'd be doing. He could just as easily have put a ball in his head or hanged himself from the yard arm. He's a military man. His job is to face death, and I'm sure he's seen more than his share, but nothing like what's happened here."

Brio shook his head. "But in the end, he's still a British officer, loyal to his flag and King. Until yesterday, he was hell bent on seeing you dead, Captain. I'm not so sure we should let him live. Who knows what turn his mind may take next."

"Aye," said Pike, "and mayhap we'd be doing him a kindness to end it for him, put him out of his torment."

"I wouldn't be too quick. We may yet need him if there's a fight to come."

"As you say, Diego," Pike said. "But he still bears watching. As does that one." Down the deck, Batteaux sat with Francine, a protective arm around her shoulders. "She might have been entranced, but he weren't. He did that monster's dirty work for him."

"But he killed him in the end. Once he thought his daughter was gone, Varlek had no more hold on him."

"No matter the reason, he still ought to pay for his crimes."

"That reckoning may yet come, but for now, we need his knowledge."

"With all due respect, Diego," said Brio, "it is like carrying a viper in your vest pocket and never knowing which time you reach for your snuff box that it may sink its fangs into your hand. He had the knowledge to send the dead Englishmen into the sea. He surely has the knowledge to make them return."

"That is a gamble we have to take. The sun is full in the sky now, we –" Across the harbor, Diego saw men on the beach. Islanders and some of Diego's crew were coming to the dock. "It looks as if our friends have been as successful as we. Send one of the men up the mast to signal them."

C

On the beach, Cataldo and Vargas stared at the burning ship. "Is that the Votrelec?" said Vargas.

"It is."

"And that is the British ship, the Avenger beyond her."

On the Avenger, a man stood in the crow's nest waving a pennon. Three passes, then two, and repeated.

"It's our people," said Vargas. "And I'll wager they're the reason the Votrelec is burning. Let's go to the Avenger."

In a short time, Cataldo, Vargas, and a half dozen men were rowing past the burning hulk. Vargas looked over his shoulder and saw Diego, Brio and Pike at the rail. "If you doubted the Hand before, Cataldo," he said. "Doubt him no more."

When Cataldo and Vargas boarded the Avenger, Batteaux and Francine were nowhere to be seen. Diego had them go into Brackenridge's cabin, for he feared Cataldo and his men would kill both of them on sight.

"So, my friend," Diego said, "You've had a time of it."

"As have you." Cataldo looked about the deck. "Where is your crew?"

"All you see here."

Cataldo looked back to the Votrelec, collapsing into itself, its main mast toppled. "I'm sure you have a story to tell."

"Indeed, but first, tell us, what of the people in the church?"

"Most are still alive. The battle was terrible, but the church is secure."

"And the invaders?"

We killed all of the white-eyes we could find. The priest is coming to destroy the *vampiri* in the coffins on the ship, but it seems the fire may have done the task for him."

"We will attend to any on the ship. The *Padre* will be needed on the land. Those vampires who did not return to the Votrelec have sought shelter in dark places. They will have to be found, as many as can be, before the sun sets. This is far from over."

Cataldo looked over his shoulder at the charred ruin of the Votrelec. "Then let us be at it."

CI

I n the hold of the Votrelec, Diego found some coffins splintered, but others intact, bobbing and bouncing in the water that filled the breached hold. They used the davit to raise the first of the coffins. "Sunlight kills them?" said Cataldo.

"So we understand," Diego replied. The sun was mid-morning high.

Cataldo wrenched the lid away, and found one of the Anointed lying stiff-limbed, eyes closed. The red eyes sprang open, and the creature's mouth gaped. It began a wailing that froze the men where they stood. The vampire's skin began to smoke, then to pop and bubble like stew in a kettle. It sat bolt upright in the coffin and would have climbed out, but Diego dangled Father Beppo's rosary before its face, and it flinched back.

"Aaaaugh!" Brackenridge screamed and rushed at the coffin, plunging his stake through the vampire's heart. It writhed for a moment, its existence suddenly revolving around an axis of wood, then its flesh sagged inward, leaving a desiccated husk.

"Bring the other coffins," said Cataldo, "and search every nook of this ship. Leave nothing alive."

CII

O n the island, Father Beppo separated the men into parties of three or four, armed them with crucifixes and stakes, and sent them to search the island, every cave, every barn, every dark place where any of the vampires might hide.

He led a party of his own to search in the trees and brush near the harbor. One of the men called out, "*Padre*, here." He was pointing at a thin mound where one of the vampires had dug a shallow grave and pulled the sand over him. Beppo crossed himself and said a brief prayer. He opened his flask and poured consecrated water over the mound.

With a shriek, the vampire in the grave came boiling out of the sand clawing and flailing. As soon as the sun struck it, its skin began to smoke. It fell to the ground, mewling, covering its face with its taloned hands and curling into a ball.

"Finish it," said the priest, holding his crucifix over the vampire.

"Let him suffer a while," snarled one of the islanders. "Bloodthirsty bastard."

"Juan," snapped Beppo. Juan's eyes met the *Padre's* piercing stare. "We are here to cleanse, not torture. Let the poor creature's soul go to its judgment."

Juan looked away, abashed, and nodded his head. "You are right, Father, I forget myself." He drove the stake through the vampire's back and out his chest. The creature screamed, shuddered, and lay still. As they watched, it shrank within itself, flesh falling from its bones until nothing was left but a skeleton in rags.

Beppo and the others crossed themselves and moved on, now the predators instead of the prey.

Raoul and his companions came to the entrance of a cave and hesitated. "Should we go in?" said Barnabus.

"We must. Light a torch."

Raoul led the way into the cave, crucifix held high before him. The ceiling lowered as they went deeper into the hillside and the men had to crouch to move further. Eyes gleamed, and suddenly a dark shape pounced on Raoul, knocking him backward and sinking its fangs into his forearm. Barnabus thrust the torch at the beast, and the jaguar bounded out of the cave and into the jungle.

They helped Raoul into the sunlight where they bound his wounds. "Shall we take you back to the village?"

Raoul shook his head. "I'm all right. Let's go on. That cat wouldn't share the cave with one of the *vampiri*. We just have to remember that there are things to beware that don't honor the cross."

In the town, men searched the root cellars, the closets, and any darkened nook they could, sometimes finding nothing, but when they found one of the anointed, they acted swiftly to dispatch the monsters. By mid afternoon, they had searched the island thoroughly.

"We must still be on our guard," said Beppo. "Some of these fiends may yet live. If they do, their lust for blood will bring them to us."

"When can we return to our homes?" one man said.

"Another day, perhaps, but at least now we can bring in food and water. Some of the white eyes may still be prowling the island, but now we know how to deal with them."

CIII

On the Votrelec, Cataldo's men opened a cupboard to find a man huddled inside covering his face with his hands. One of them pointed a stake at his chest. "Please. I'm not one of those things. I'm human. Don't kill me. Varlek took me captive." Cataldo hauled him from his hiding place and banged him against the bulkhead. Holding him by the throat with one hand, Cataldo put a cross in his face with the other.

"You want to be spared? Kiss the Savior."

The captive pursed his lips and bent his head forward, but at the last instant turned his face away. Without hesitation, Cataldo dropped the icon, took the man's head in both hands, and wrenched it over his shoulder.

On deck, Diego and the others built a pyre of the coffins and threw the grisly remains of the vampires on it. Cataldo came from the hold with a corpse over his shoulder. "One of Varlek's human lackeys," he said, throwing the body on the heap with the vampires.

The men poured oil on the wood, and Diego dry fired his pistol for the spark to set it aflame.

The men stood as the fire climbed higher. Diego turned to Brackenridge, who stared rapt at the blazing pyre.

"Are you satisfied?" Diego said.

Brackenridge turned to stare into Diego's eyes. "I will never be satisfied."

CIV

Father Beppo decided that the flock should go outside the church but not yet return to their homes, in case some of the *trúdovi* might still be roaming nearby.

"Is it safe, Father?" one of the women asked him, clutching the hands of two small children.

"It is as safe as we are vigilant, my child."

Cataldo's men brought the freed children ashore in their boats to tearful reunions with their surviving relatives.

On the deck of the Avenger, Diego stood watching the last of the

Votrelec as it burned, its evil following the smoke that billowed upward into the cloudless sky. With no warning, he felt cold steel against the back of his head and heard the cocking of a pistol.

"Diego lo Mano, by the authority vested in me by the Crown, I arrest you on the charge of piracy. Surrender your weapons."

Diego raised empty hands and turned slowly to see the madness in Brackenridge's eyes. "Have I not atoned for my many sins by my part in saving the people of the Exiles, stopping Varlek, and giving you your vengeance on those who killed your crew?"

"The law is the law," the Englishman said. "Duty compels me. Your guilt and its degree will be determined by the judiciary in Kingston, where –"

His last thought was cut off when Pike laid a belaying pin across the back of his head.

"You were right to watch him, Pike. Let's take him ashore."

CV

At the church, Diego, Cataldo, and Father Beppo spoke to the islanders grouped in the courtyard. "We have driven back the evil," said Beppo, "but perhaps not completely. We must be watchful, especially at night, that none of these devils returns." The bodies of the *trúdovi* and of the vampires had been gathered in the courtyard and wood piled around them. A small brazier of red coals stood beside it.

"Each of you, man, woman and child, take a brand from the fire and throw it onto this unholy pyre. Each of you take a hand in its destruction, and know that you have had a hand in its end." The flames were small and slow at first, but by the time the last of the islanders had thrown in his burning twig, the flames were high and hot, destroying the last vestiges of the unholy attackers.

"And what will you do now?" Cataldo asked Diego.

"What we always do. If you will provision my ship, we will sail with the next tide and you'll be rid of us."

"And him?" Cataldo jerked his head to Brackenridge, who sat sullen, hands in manacles.

"Free him as soon as we sail. At our next port, we'll get word to the Admiralty that one of their ships is stranded here and needs a crew."

"I still say we should scuttle her," grumbled Pike. "Or someday she'll be barking up our arse again."

"You can count on that, lo Mano," Brackenridge said, his eyes blazing. "I welcome the challenge."

Vargas approached from the shore. "The Belladonna is entering the harbor, Captain." Diego had sent his men earlier to the other side of the island to retrieve his ship from the cove.

Diego nodded. "Soon, we will be gone and your lives can go on, perhaps not as they once did, but they will go on."

"And Varlek's man and his daughter?" Cataldo demanded.

"They go with us. We'll let them off where they can book passage home. I believe he has acquitted himself."

"Yes," said Beppo. "I have heard his confession, and he is absolved of sin."

Cataldo grunted with dissatisfaction, but said no more.

"You have done the Lord's work, my son," Father Beppo said to Diego, "and I thank you. I would say, 'go your way and sin no more,' but I know better."

"A rogue by any other name," Diego said with a laugh. He looked to Cataldo and again to the priest. "But in all your learning and experience, *Padre*, has there ever been a stranger Trinity?"

The End

ABOUT OUR CREATORS

Writer:

FRED ADAMS, JR. is a retired Penn State University English Professor who spends his days writing pulp fiction and his nights working as a singer-songwriter. His Sam Dunne novel *Dead Man's Melody* was nominated as Pulp Novel of the Year in 2017's Pulp Factory Awards, and his Smith Brothers novel *The Eye of Quang-Chi* was nominated for the same award in 2018. His titles include *Hitwolf* 1 and 2, *Six Gun Terrors* vols. 1, 2, and 3, and *C.O. Jones: Mobsters and Monsters, Skinners,* and *The Damned and the Doomed*. His original Sherlock Holmes anthology *The Affair of the Chronic Argonaut* was recently published by Pro Se Press. Forthcoming titles from Airship 27 include *C.O. Jones: Home Front, Six Gun Terrors 4: The Town Killers*, a Sam Dunne Mystery, *Blood is the New Black*, and *Holster Full of Death*, a Dead Sheriff novel. He lives in Mount Pleasant, Pennsylvania in "perpetual terror of boredom."

Visit Fred's website at http://drphreddee.com/author

Illustrator:

ROB DAVIS—began his professional art career doing illustrations for role-playing games in the late 1980s. Not long after he began lettering and inking, then penciling comics for a number of small black and white comics publishers- most notably for Eternity Comics, which eventually became Malibu Comics in the 1990s, on their book SCIMIDAR with writer R.A. Jones. Expanding his career he eventually began working at both DC and Marvel on likeness intensive comics like adaptations from TV shows like QUANTUM LEAP and STAR TREK's many incarnations. Primarily he worked on the DEEP SPACE NINE comics for Malibu. At Marvel he worked on the comics adaptation of Saturday morning cartoon PIRATES OF DARK WATER. After the comics industry implosion in the late 1990's Rob picked up work on video games, advertising illustration and T-shirt design as well as some small press comics like ROBYN OF SHERWOOD for Caliber.

Rob continues to do the occasional self-published comic book as well as publisher and designer for his small-press production REDBUD STUDIO COMICS. Rob is Art Director, Designer and Illustrator for the New Pulp production partnership AIRSHIP 27 collaborating with writer/editor Ron Fortier. Rob is the recipient of the PULP FACTORY AWARD for "Best Interior Illustrations" in 2010 and 2016 for his work on SHERLOCK HOLMES: CONSULTING DETECTIVE and has been nominated for the same award a number of times since. A collection of selected Rob's illustrations from Airship 27 has been published as PULP: THE ART OF ROB DAVIS available at Amazon.com and Barnes & Noble online with a second collection in the planning stages. He works and lives in Missouri with his wife and two children.

Cover Artist

ADAM BENET SHAW –Accomplished painter, illustrator, and comics creator, Adam has garnered acclaim across a number of artistic media. After completing studies at the Cleveland Institute of Art in Ohio, the Edinburgh College of Art in Scotland and Watts Atelier in California, Shaw was selected as an emerging American artist to watch by European gallery owners and exhibited in London, England. He has been featured in "New American Painting", selected multiple times for the Arkansas Art Center's Delta Exhibit, and shown at the prestigious "Red Clay Survey" at the Huntsville Museum of Art. His work has also been shown in over 50 group and solo shows in the US and internationally.   His figurative paintings are a prominent part of a 140-foot mural entitled "The History of Cotton" at the National Cotton Exchange Museum, St. Jude's Children's Research Hospital, the National Contact Bridge Museum, and a treasured part of private and corporate collections. He has created storyboards for several motion pictures, including Paramount Pictures' film "Black Snake Moan" directed by Craig Brewer, stage design for operas and corporate events, and character illustrations for the gaming industry. His published graphic novel work includes the series "Dead In Memphis", "Bloodstream" for Image Comics, "David: The Illustrated Novel" from Shepherd King Publishing and "Harpe: America's First Serial Killers" from Cave-in-Rock Publishing. He shares his love of art through teaching and workshops at his studio in the Broad Avenue Arts District in Memphis. Recently he has been painting book covers for pulp publishers Pro Se Productions and Airship 27 Productions.

BOOKS BY FRED ADAMS JR.

FRED ADAMS JR. PULP WRITER

SIX-GUN TERRORS Volume One
SIX-GUN TERRORS   Volume Two
SIX-GUN TERRORS Volume Three – The Slithering Terror

HITWOLF
HITWOLF 2 – The Pack

C.O. JONES
C.O. JONES – Skinners
C.O. JONES – The Damned and the Doomed

(SAM DUNNE MYSTERIES)
Dead Man's Melody
Blood is the New Black

(THE SMITH BROTHERS SERIES)
The Eye of Quang Chi

(IKE MARS MYSTERIES)
The Bloody Key

Fangs of the Sea

Find these and other great pulp-style books at airship27hangar.com

FRED ADAMS JR.
PULP WRITER

A former Vietnam Green Beret becomes a werewolf hitman for the New Jersey mob. A private eye struck twice by lightning discovers he can mold his face like rubber and disguise himself to look like other people. Con joined Chinese-American twin brothers solve crimes in San Francisco at the turn of the 20th century. These are only a few of the remarkable, unique and amazing characters you will discover in this collection of six pulp stories from the imagination of Fred Adams Jr. The wonder starts here!

FRED ADAMS JR.
PULP WRITER

PULP FICTION FOR A NEW GENERATION!

AN AIRSHIP 27 PRODUCTION

AIRSHIP27HANGAR.COM

NEW PULP

A Sampler of all-new stories from:
HITWOLF · SIX-GUN TERRORS · C.O. JONES
IKE MARS · THE SMITH BROTHERS · SAM DUNNE

www.ingramcontent.com/pod-product-compliance
Lightning Source LLC
Chambersburg PA
CBHW051145260626
47170CB00005B/1964